benny

... he wants to be a monk!

a comic novel   by Jim Cronin

50 high street
Croton-on-Hudson
New York 10520
Copyright 2010
914 271 8812
jimcronin50@verizon.net

*Our mission is to efficiently provide the world's finest, most comprehensive book publishing
service, enabling every author to experience success. To find out how to publish your
book, your way, and have it available worldwide, visit us online at www.trafford.com*

Trafford rev. 09/30/2010

 www.trafford.com

North America & international
toll-free: 1 888 232 4444 (USA & Canada)
phone: 250 383 6864 ✦ fax: 812 355 4082

BENNY

Cast of Characters

Benny	A guy from Queens
Albert	A priest from St Sebastians
Mo	Benny's brother
Ma	Benny's mother
Rodney	The Spirit of St Sebastians
Big Leo	A Queens business man
Marko	An employee of Big Leo
Felix	Another employee of Big Leo
Fiddler	Another employee of Big Leo
Angel	A Queens business man
Irish	An employee of Angel
Goldie	Another employee of Angel
Dave	An advertising man
Baby	Dave's squeeze and Marko's sister
Psychiatrist	
The Cardinal	

benny

Benny lived in Queens. He was 26 years old. So far he had done nothing in his life that he could stand up and shout about. He was bored and he would say, about himself, loud and drawn out B - O - R - E –D. He lived in the same row house he was born in - over on 226th street. He also lived with the same mother and the same father - until he died two years ago at age 68 . Mo his younger brother lived there too - one happy family.

But brother, Mo, had a real career he was a plumber and in today's crazy world that was likened to owning a gold mine. Mo could walk into a leaking house and in three hours walk out about $300 richer and the owners of the house couldn't stop thanking him. His father had set Mo up for a plumbing career but Benny turned down the same opportunity to take a white collar job in the city where the only people he ever met were those spending their days staring at a computer screen just like him.

Nine to five everyday meant Benny would look at one set of figures then another set of figures then another set of figures then the computer would tell him what the health insurance of some company was going to cost. He had to answer complaints all day long. He would direct one small business to a new insurance company in the morning then have to call them back in the afternoon because the place they were directed to suddenly raised their rates or went out of business. And calls from individuals were killing him. He couldn't stand the crying woman whose dying daughter could no longer get insurance. The real trouble was that every one who spoke to him seemed like they were blaming him personally for their problems, Benny would keep telling them, "I agree with you that the company should not be doing what they were doing but it's not my fault."

He kept a log pinned to the wall of his cubicle listing the number of times he had been called a bastard or worse. And another column which called him a traitor for saying he sympathized with them and still kept working for the lousy company. When he went home that Friday the score was 118 unreasonable bastards or worse and 52 traitors. Not the best way to end a week but thanking god out loud that it was the end of the week.

He did have Saturdays off and he could spend them like he did for twenty years at the cigar shop on the corner. It really was a cigar shop but it hardly sold cigars anymore. Chester, the 78 year old owner, lived on magazine, candy, newspaper, lottery tickets, soda, beer to go, ready made sandwiches, and cigarette sales. He was happy. Saturdays Benny would hang out there and give Chester time off for the bathroom or whatever. When Chester stepped out Benny stepped to the magazine rack and began a review of all the magazines that had arrived since his last visit. When Chester announced he was going to be away for an hour or more Benny would break the seal (being careful to glue it back after he had his looks) on some of the more risqué magazines and look at the young ladies in their exotic poses. He was reading or looking at one of these this day and spotted the Ad which said,

> BORED
> *Try a New Life!*
> *Join the order of St Sebastian.*
> *No experience necessary –*
> *Just a love of God*
> *Are you willing to take a chance*
> *on changing your life.*
> *Visit St. Sebastian*
> *Only an hour and a half drive from New York –*
> *Off the Taconic parkway at Butternut Road*
> *Visit us Today!*
> *Three miles on the left*

Benny felt that God and the magazine was talking to him.

Chester returned and Benny talked with him for a time. Chester was a cinch to complain about prices – the price of rent - the price of 2 cent candy which was now a dime – the heating bill – the air conditioning bill – the stupid way the government did – well, just about everything. And he talked about Joe Torre like it was his fault that A-Rod struck out on a great pitch and Jeter was not getting a hit every time he came to bat.

Benny took a Kit Kat bar as payment for baby-sitting the store and then took a lone walk. He thought about a lot of things. He finally got around to thinking about Sr. Alberta who scared him into worrying about Heaven and Hell. He knew she would have hated the insurance business. Then he thought about Mr. Simons, his ninth grade teacher, who always stuck in his mind as a man who wanted to do more and more with his life for other people. Mr. Simons spent all his summers in Africa helping the people there.

Benny thought about his career, brief as it was, as an altar boy. He liked being on the altar with the priest – he felt as if people looked up to him. He might have stayed an altar boy for years more but Wally Nutter drank all the wine back in the sacristy while he was there with him. Father O'Neill blew his stack and gave Wally hell and Benny got fired from the altar boy life for being with Wally and 'letting him do it.' There was no sense in thinking about his mother's reaction to this. She told Benny "such a sin as this would be with him forever for stealing the wine that was to become the blood of the savior of the world and gulping it down like a common drunk."

For months later he felt condemned to hell fire until he met Joe. Joe was a brother in a Catholic order and he made sense out of a lot of things. He taught love rather than fear, and with Joe, Heaven or at least a decent life after death, was possible. He made Benny realize that a close relationship with God was not a 'sissy' thing but a real 'macho' thing. He always talked about saints who were nothing but ordinary people who spent their lives doing something good. And most of them had taken steps to change their life from boredom to activity for God.

Benny walked into the kitchen while his mother was making lasagna and told her he was going to join the priesthood – she fainted and spilled sauce all over her chest.

Mo walked in and screamed , " My God, you've killed her – you've killed Mom!"

"That's red sauce, but she might not recover – I just told her I was going to become a priest – and..."

"You what?"

"I told her I was going to become a priest."

"Look. Benny, you don't have to do that. I can speak to the union chief and you can be a plumber."

Ma started to stir and she saw all the sauce on her, "Am I bleeding? What did you do Benny?"

"It's only the sauce, Ma, you're all right."

Mo went to her and started helping her up, she started mumbling, "Benny just said he was going to become a priest, Mo, why should he tell me such a thing?"

"It's true Ma, Hold her Mo." She started slipping down again.

Twenty minutes later, the sauce was picked up, Ma was shaking, but sitting at the table, Benny and Mo sat with her calmly.

"Benny, it may be a stupid question, but how did you decide on this, remember, you drank the wine. The precious wine that was supposed to become the blood of Christ until you drank it – how can you become a priest after such a thing. I still pray you can get into heaven for doing such a thing."

"I just want to do it. And God will forgive me for the wine.?"

"But not Father O'Neill!"

Mo spoke up, "Ma, Father O'Neill, sells suits at Bloomingdale's – he doesn't consecrate wine any more."

"But he did."

* *

MANHATTAN

Albert pulled his silver 2002 Camry into the underground parking Space. He hated the whole idea of parking in New York. The last 30 minutes he made right turn after right turn looking for a space, but as he would have guessed there was none. Now he would have to pay $30.00 to meet for a few minutes with Dave. Dave's agency would pay for the lunch but not the parking.

Albert was born in Peke's Falls in upstate New York along the Erie Canal – his backyard was the canal and just a few hundred feet from the Peke's Lock. Albert remembered how he and his 'gang' would often sit and watch the boats rise to a new level and continue on the canal or to a lower level and continue. The boats were so close to the canal's edge that you could touch them as the moved by. Touching them was a big taboo and the seamen on the boat would holler the kids away.

When Albert was fifteen he got is first paying job in Mr. Potter's nursery. His first duties were wrapping the Christmas plants in clay pots with red or green foil – a Christmas look. After the season Mr. Potter gave Albert another job in the nursery watering the new plants and keeping the nursery clean. When Mr. Potter gave Albert the job of planting seeds for the Easter plants, he started thinking of a career in horticulture. He remembers not knowing what that word meant but his father explained it to him. The idea of dropping a tiny seed into fresh dirt and then to see the green buds come poking through and rising as tall stately flowers fascinated Albert.

Albert never became a gardener or horticulturist but he always thought the sight and wonder of the growing flowers, together with short, stocky, feisty Sister Agnes, moved him to the priesthood. After high school he registered in Avon College a small college nearby and after a year of discerning he entered a junior seminary. Soon after he began his studies he asked for and received permission to join the Order of St. Sebastians. St. Sebastians was near his home and he wanted to be close to his folks who were aging fast and most likely would need help in the near future. They passed away a few years ago both within a year of each other.

Now Albert was alone – really alone.

The attendant gestured to him and handed him a ticket, " Have a nice day, Father." He would have a nicer day if he didn't have to pay the $30.00 for parking. There was a time, years ago, Albert could hardly remember how long ago, when his Roman Collar might get him a free ride – but no more. A priest today was just a regular ordinary guy.

* *

The cubes in the martini glass began to rattle and roll– beads of sweat formed on his forehead – his knees grew weak – he wasn't sure he could stand - but he really didn't want to – he wanted to leave the "21" and go die.

Dave had learned to drink on the job. The job was an account executive on a batch of small accounts Whippet Ad Agency had put together.   When he graduated six years ago from college he was sure he was going to be the man Madison Avenue had waited all its 'ad' life for. All his professors at Pine Tree College had faith in him and they assured him he was going to make it big on Madison Avenue.

The Whippet agency wasn't even on Madison Avenue - it was on 47th Street.

Every year Dave took his client, Father Albert of St Sebastian's , one of Dave's small accounts - billing only $350,000 – ergo - only one lunch a year . Dave had the Art Department put together a few boards on what they would be doing in the next year and Fr. Albert was thrilled with them.

Although his agency and he did not make a lot of profit on the St Sebastian account Dave had always felt it was a kind of contribution to the good of society.

Dave asked, "Tell me father as a result of our campaign last year what was the increase in vocations?

Fr. Albert replied "Zero."

"You mean it ran flat all last year."

"No, it ran Zero."

"What do you mean Zero?"

"That is the amount of vocations we got last year."

Dave sipped a fresh martini and asked, "What do you mean?"

"I mean, Dave, nobody joined the order – nobody."

That was when the ice cubes started to rattle louder and sweat appeared and Dave stammered, "You mean all the ads we ran – these beautiful brochures – we did not get one person to join. Not one teeny weeny one."

"That is correct."

"We have to do something about it. Increase our budget and move to an increase in full color brochures – instead of four we'll have eight. There are men out there who want to join and we have to reach them."

"I don't think so."

"What do you mean?"

"I think no more campaigns. St. Sebastian is not prepared to spend its last few hundred thousand. Father Robert, who was with me at the founding of St Sebastian's died during the year and now I am the only priest left in the order. I can stay open for a few months more then I will close. I have to place the remaining monies in an account to take care of all the closing expenses which will be expensive"

Dave was shaking. He really couldn't believe that he had failed – that the campaign had failed – that Sebastian's was in danger of closing.

Father Albert smiled, "It's not your fault Dave. No one is getting very many vocations. Some orders that could measure their incoming classes in the hundreds are now down to a dozen or less. A friend of mine was telling me that his community ordained one man last year and he was 59. That one man means there are a total of nine in the whole monastery. Don't worry Dave – it is bad now but it will be all right in the future."

"Where will you go – what will you do?"

"Remember, I am a priest and from what I see jobs are pretty easy to come by for a guy like me. I have seven offers already."

"But what about St. Sebastians – what happens to that?"

"As the last surviving member of the order – I will dispose of it in some fashion. Sell it most likely and give the proceeds to the church and the poor."

Dave was listening to Albert and slowly nodding his head up and down agreeing with him. At least his boss will not be screaming at him – the lack of priests - St. Sebastians is a common dilemma – but Dave never dreamed it was as bad as Albert was describing.

Albert rose from the table, "Well, thanks for the lunch, Dave. I hope we can meet again some time, I appreciate your comments from Shakespeare, but these yearly reviews are over. And the art work and 'sell' in these brochures is really great and I do appreciate it – but we are finished."

Dave rose and shook Albert's hand, " Thanks, Albert, and good luck."

Albert turned and left. Dave sank slowly into his chair and ordered a peach martini so he could relax.

* *

QUEENS

Word of Benny's big decision was all over the neighborhood before Ma got the red sauce wiped off her blouse.

Benny had wanted to keep it low key and just tell a few people but that was not possible. Right in the middle of wiping the red sauce off, Lucy, their cousin from across the street walked in and wanted to know what happened to Ma.

MO smiled at her and spoke, "Benny just told Ma he was going to become a priest and Ma fainted."

"Is he all right?"

"Sure she's fine."

She pointed at Benny." I don't mean her I meant him!"

"Yeah, I'm alright. What's the big deal?"

She blessed herself three times and walked out

MO, stared after her, "Now the world knows."

Well, it doesn't have to be a secret and besides I didn't even sign up or let anybody know I was coming."

"Where?"

Benny showed Mo the ad from the magazine.

"Just drive up the Taconic and..."

The phone rang.

Ma picked it up and nodded, "That's right. Lucy was right. A real priest. Maybe he'll even be right here at Sacred Heart. Sure we'll have a party. I'll talk more about it tomorrow. Good night."

She hung up the phone and then it rang again. "Hello... That's right...

No...it wasn't me..." she held the phone against her chest, " Mrs. Green wants to know whose idea it was?"

"Mine." And Benny slumped into a chair and shook his head.

"He says it was his idea...maybe the Catholic School he went to...

That night there were a total of 17 phone calls about Benny's big decision.

* *

THE GOING AWAY PARTY

First they wanted to have the party in the Sacred Heart Church basement, but it was quickly ruled out when the pastor discovered there might be more to drink than just wine and beer. Mo booked Monahan's bar and lounge over on 231st street. It was not a bad place and lots of families in the neighborhood were there on Friday nights for $5.95 specials. It was a favorite place to have a few drinks during the week and there were hardly any fights. The room in the back was made for parties of 50 people but they crammed at least 100 Benny lovers into it.

Fr. Finnegan was there and Benny couldn't believe it but somebody had resurrected Sister Alberta who sat in the corner swilling beer. Benny's mother and brother MO, cousins from the Bronx, two relatives from New Jersey, and a few guys from Benny's work in Manhattan were mixed among the neighborhood people.

Fr. Finnegan was the first to stand and give a toast," to one of the finest and most religious young men our parish has ever produced – drink up. Benny smiled, Finnegan, had knuckled him on the head about fifty times and swore that he was going the way of Satan

Sister Alberta was helped to her feet by a companion nun and held up a bottle of Sam Adams, "to Benny, the young boy I spotted early in his career that he would surely be a priest – how did I know this?

I knew because he always wore a medal honoring the Blessed Mother and he loved to read the Bible – drink up." Most of the people clapped and she plopped down. Benny had no idea who she was talking about - he knew it couldn't be him.

Arnie was taking bets in the corner. It was 8 to 5 he wouldn't last a month and 16 to one he wouldn't stay a year.

Girls were talking about celibacy and virginity in another corner and what was the difference? Benny did not want to get into that discussion – especially since he was pretty intimate, to say the least, with some of the girls.

Benny's mother was holding court with a group of her friends admitting that it was a bit of surprise when Benny announced his decision. "He just walked in while I was working in the kitchen and told me what he decided. I was stunned. He hardly goes to church – he is always oversleeping. I hope he knows what he is doing."

Benny's hope that he could just slip away and try it for a time was slipping away. He was beginning to think he would have no chance to quit the pressure was too great.

The shaking hands to receive the congratulations, the meatballs and sausage, but mostly the good Brooklyn Beer and he could hardly keep on his feet. He decided if he was going to be there at the end of the party he better get some rest. He found a room with a couch in it that must have been the owner's spot and he went inside to lie down for a few minutes. He fell asleep.

He was awakened by the smell of cheap perfume. He opened his eyes and lying on top of him, was Sally Ripon, the waitress. He raised his head a bit and Sally was naked. He shook his head and tried to get up, but she clung to him.

"What the hell are you doing?"

"I'm your going away present."

11

"My going away present? I'm going away to become a priest."

"They told me that then they told me to be sure and not hold anything back."

"I can't do this – it's wrong."

"Who sez?" and she began to gently move up and down on his body.

He became aroused in spades. He tried to hold himself back. "But we can't...

"Sure we can." And she started covering his body with kisses.

Benny was stuck – He wanted to and he didn't want to "They'll bust in and surprise us."

"They can't – the door is being guarded."

He slipped off his pants and Sally never stopped working on him.

He heard Mrs. Armstrong talking to his mother on the other side of the door.

"You have got to be so proud of your Benny – becoming a priest – I wish my son, Chuck, would consider the priesthood."

"If only Chuck were here now – Benny could talk to him and maybe who knows." Their voices trailed off and as much as Benny knew Chuck – he knew Chuck would give anything to be here right now in this very place where Benny was.

Sally performed nobly and Benny had sex he never dreamed possible.

Benny was lying exhausted on the couch.

Sally was getting dressed, "That was real fun Benny – enjoy yourself as a priest and I can hardly wait to go to confession to you – Bye now." And she left.

* *

Benny left three days after the going away party. He had to wait until he completely recovered. Sally Ripon was one thing but then the guys came back in and dressed Benny. They gave him a pillowcase to walk around and hold in front of people. He could hardly walk let alone carry a pillowcase. Wally, the drinking altar boy, helped him and he collected money in the pillowcase. Everybody wished him well and asked for his prayers and threw $5 (or more) in the pillowcase. Finally he went to bed at 5 A.M. with a very bad headache, an explosive stomach and a pillowcase with $642 in it.

The ride up the Taconic was not bad at all – he enjoyed the fields and low mountains and patches of flowers on the way. It was a beautiful country. He pondered St. Sebastians – what would it be like? – What were the guys he would meet be like? Should he have called first? Would they send him to some kind of school? Supposing they didn't take him? If that happened he had to give the $642 back and the pillowcase was in the trunk of his Corolla just in case. He had no idea of who gave what – but he'd still have to do it somehow. Some of the older people lavished rosary beads on him – he now had twelve.

One lady gave him a thing called scapulars – When he told her he didn't know what they were, she smiled and said "You will, Benny, you will."

Were there other surprises for him? Half of him wanted a lot of surprises – when he got back to Queens someday people would be amazed at what he knew. Maybe. The other half of him was scared as hell of surprises and what they could do to him. He heard stories of the seminary and the way students had to endure lots of hazing and crazy things. If he listened to his pal Wally the place was like a dungeon where torture was the order of the day.

Butternut road. He turned off the Taconic. Three miles on the left there it was "St. Sebastians." He passed through a big gate and there in front of him was a huge building. He was impressed. He drove on a circular drive around the building to see where the cars were parked. He saw none. Finally he chose a spot near what looked to be the front door. There were several doors around the big red brick building but this one seemed a little bigger and more ornate than the others. He got out of the car – he decided to leave his bag in the car until he had directions of where to put it.

He walked up the steps leading to the front door and rang the bell.

He looked around - it was a beautiful spot. The gardens were all neat and the small trees trimmed – he imagined all the students working on the grounds to keep it neat. There were various paths leading off into the woods and others heading down towards what he believed was a small lake. He rang the bell again. He could hear it ringing and it carried a sort of echo. Five minutes more and three more rings still nobody answered. He didn't know what to do. He checked the ad in is pocket and this was the place. What could he do? Would he have to go back and tell the gang he wanted to be a priest but nobody was home.

When he was about to quit a car drove up and parked next to his.

A man, about 60, got out and waved to him.

"Can I help you?"

"I've been ringing the bell and nobody seems to answer."

"Are you looking for someone? Maybe I can help."

"I have this Ad I picked up at Chester's cigar shop and I was thinking I would like to join this...this order here and become a priest. This is St Sebastian's isn't it?"

"This is St Sebastian's and I am Father Albert. I live here."

Benny looked at him. He wasn't dressed any different than a plain man. "You don't look like one."

"One what?"

"A Priest."

"You mean I don't wear a roman collar, or have a long cassock, or a brown robe similar to a Franciscan Monk. I wear some of those things for special occasions but not everyday."

"Father Finnegan wouldn't be caught dead without a full outfit on. He's my pastor."

"Good for Father Finnegan. But you - you would like to join the order of St. Sebastian."

"Yeah, the ad said to come and try it – so here I am." Benny was not sure of the right words to use with the priest, who didn't dress like one. Maybe this was a big shot in the order and he had a special name like 'your excellency' or 'your potentate' and maybe he should be kneeling or kissing his ring or something like that.

Albert looked suspiciously at Benny – was he for real? Or was he some wise kid just testing the ad. Albert couldn't believe he was for real – it had never happened before and why happen today of all days – it wasn't the feast of St Sebastian – that wasn't until January – it was just another day. Albert thought about the admonition of many saints that the "spirit acts in strange ways," – just a few days ago he canceled all the ads and BANG in walks a candidate who answered an old ad.

Benny felt awkward and embarrassed, "What do I call you?"

"Albert, that's my name."

"Is it 'Father' or "Bishop' or anything like that."

"Just Albert – that's good enough – No one calls me Father anymore and I am not a Bishop."

"Just Albert? Are you sure?"

"I'm sure. Are you hungry?"

"A little. What time do we eat here?"

"We'll go out for pizza – c'mon." He gestured for Benny to get in his car.

"What about my stuff?"

"Leave it. It's safe."

15

Benny hesitated, shrugged his shoulder, and got into Albert's car.

* *

Albert took Benny to a small restaurant about three miles away.

Sal's Tavern was about three miles from St Sebastians in a small strip mall. The main village was another two miles away, but Sal's was a favorite Pizza place for many miles around. Albert was describing the wonderful Pizza that Sal's made. He ordered one big pie and after checking with Benny ordered two draft beers.

Benny sized up the place. It was small a few booths along two walls and four tables in the center. There were several Beer signs on the walls, a big picture of a fire engine, with a whole lot of signatures criss-crossing over it and a big 'Thanks Sal' scrawled over the whole thing.

Albert noticed Benny turning his face one way and the other trying to read names on the picture.

"We had a big fire a couple of years ago..."

Benny interrupted, "At the seminary?"

"No, not at the seminary but at a big old house in town and the firemen, all volunteers, fought it all day, so Sal gave sent down free pizza. The firemen gave the picture to Sal in thanks. That is the kind of the way things happen in small towns."

Benny nodded, "It was a nice thing to do, back home in Queens we don't really get a chance to do something like that – the firemen are all employees and can't really take favors. That is the kind of the way it is in the big city."

Albert smiled and liked the way this young man was handling himself, "What made you decide to visit us?"

Benny answered," The ad."

Albert smiled within himself, just a few days ago, he had fired the ad agency – the reason no results – and now like magic a 'result'. Albert figured that God or the Spirit or something had a great sense of humor. Of course this young man was far - far - from becoming a priest but he had taken the first step – a step nobody had taken at St. Sebastians in more than five years.

The pizzas arrived and the beers were refilled.

They jockeyed a piece off the pie and using napkins and paper plates started eating. After he swallowed his first piece, Benny said, "not bad. Come to Queens and you can compare it with Billy Izo's pies – his are a little more spicy."

Albert nodded, "I'll do that."

They ate in silence for a time then after his second piece Albert asked, "But what made you want to become a brother of St Sebastian. Have you thought about it for a long time."

Benny bit two more pieces off, "Yeah, I think so. It seems that one thing after another was not happening too good in Queens so I wanted a big change. I always think of this Sr. Alberta who taught me in seventh grade – she was tough, but she kept putting the "priest bug' in my ear and I always prayed about it. You know, mostly out of a kind of sense of fear that I might be punished if I didn't think about it. So the ad hit me between the eyes and it became pretty clear that I should try to get closer to God and tell other people about Him or Her. It was like my prayers were answered." He took a long drink of beer, " But you tell me about St. Sebastian. I don't even know if I ever heard of the guy."

St Sebastian was a martyr – do you know what a martyr is?"

"Sr. Alberta always claimed she was one – but really it's a guy who gives up his life for Jesus on the spot."

"Well back to St. Sebastian- he was martyred around 350 AD. One of my favorite stories about him is that at the time of the Diocletius when many Christians were being called to Martyrdom he joined the Roman Army so he could assist the martyrs without arousing suspicion. He was found out and dragged before

Emperor Diocletian. Diocletian had him delivered to his archers to be shot to death. His body was pierced by arrows. There are many paintings of him lying with his body pierced by many arrows. He was left for dead but when the men came to bury him he was found to be alive. He recovered from all the arrow wounds and was offered the chance to get out of town, so to speak, but he refused. Instead he would stand by the roadside and mock the Emperor whenever he passed. This was a little much and the Emperor ordered him killed. He was beaten to death with clubs and this time it took."

Benny had listened quietly, "Guy had a lot of guts."

Albert continued, "Legends about these early saints may not be literally true, but they do express the faith and courage evident in the lives of these heroes and heroines of Christ. To the point that all the great writers of the Church praise them and in that praise offer a kind of proof of their lives."

Benny was quiet for a time – he ate two pieces of pizza, "Not bad pizza, but it don't make it in Queens."

"I'll have to visit Queens someday. I have to admit about 99% of my impression of New York is Manhattan."

Benny nodded, "But why did you call your outfit St. Sebastian?"

Alfred ordered another beer for the two of them. "I'm guessing that the family who willed the property to Father Lucas, our founder, had something to do with it. Their family name was Riener. Jacob Riener was the head of the family and he met Father Lucas and offered him the land and the estate of about 500 acres, to establish a new order of priests. This was about 1830. He told Father Lucas that his wife had just lost a child at birth and his name was to be Sebastian. So Father Lucas called us the order of St. Sebastian in his honor."

Benny nodded, "Makes sense. I guess I'll find out a lot more about the order after I'm here a while."

Albert smiled and agreed with him. Albert was thinking how he would explain to Benny that there was no one else in that big building but the two of them. There were no other members of the order left – they had all left or died. Albert was about to initiate the papers for the Archdiocese that the Order was going to close down.

Benny wanting to join the community was interrupting that whole procedure.

Albert thought that Benny was a nice kid who was probably like a lot of other kids in the world who wanted to help others. The papers were filled everyday with starvation, wars, killings, and these kids just wanted to get away from all that. Or better wanted to get involved in solving all that craziness in a different way.

Albert decided to stick with Benny. He would give him a real reality check – on what the true state of St. Sebastian was and on what the true state of being a priest was. Albert was the official director of novices, the new men entering St. Sebastians, and the Superior General of the Order. As the last surviving member of the order he could stay open if he pleased and or sell everything off if he pleased.

They finished the pizza and beer and left.

As they drove onto the property Benny remarked "I guess everybody's asleep and they forgot to leave a light on for us."

Albert nodded, "That's what happens." He would break the news to Benny that there was no one else in the morning.

Albert led Benny to a side door and turned on a hall light and led Benny to the guest room they kept on the first floor. "Sleep here tonight, Benny, we'll get another room tomorrow."

Benny shrugged. It made no difference to him. "This place is sure quiet – not like Queens."

"Good for sleeping, Benny."

"Yeah, I guess." He dropped his bag and plopped onto the bed. "I'll see you in the morning – Father...er Albert. Good night."

Albert closed the door and left. He wouldn't sleep much thinking about what he would have to explain in the morning.

Albert and Benny were sitting in the main kitchen of the monastery – they were finishing a breakfast of English Muffins and coffee. Albert spent the whole time explaining to Benny the truth of St. Sebastians and the fact that they were the only two people there. Benny had taken it pretty good and had remained silent the whole time. Albert refilled his coffee cup and looked at Benny. Benny was still silent.

"Well, Benny, what do you think now?"

"The ad didn't say anything about a going out of business sale."

"The ad was placed before the decision was made.

" Yeah sure."

Benny leaned back and was silent. Then after what seemed like five minutes to Albert he spoke, "The pizza wasn't bad last night and you seem like an all-right- guy. So, if I wanted to stay and help you what would you do?"

Albert smiled to himself, he really liked all his first impressions of this boy, "Well, I could put off the closing and start giving you an idea of theology, I am a teacher, talk to you about what it is to be a priest, then if you continue to be interested. I could move you to an ongoing seminary and you would after several years become a priest. Whether it is in the Order of St. Sebastians or not - I am not sure."

"I really want to try it. Let' s do it."

"Let's take a walk, Benny>"

And they took the first of many walks.

* *

For the next 6 weeks while Benny stayed at St Sebastian's – he learned to cook simple meals, gardening for flowers and vegetables, how to serve mass. He was the altar boy for Albert in his everyday mass and there was something about it that was drawing Benny in – he liked it more and more. He did a lot of soul searching by himself - walking around the property and getting to know it like he had lived there for a long time. Albert even taught him to fish at the small pond on the property and even in the Hudson River. Albert would speak to him about the New Testament and the Old Testament – they were like classes - but not really. On weekends Albert would say a Sunday mass in a nearby town and Benny would often serve as his Altar Boy. After Mass there was a big breakfast and then back to the monastery and watch sports. At night they would go out to a movie or at least go out for another meal. Benny liked the routine and he could feel himself getting closer to living in a monastery forever.

* *

Albert and Benny were sitting in a grove of pine trees a short walk from the main building. Albert was having the first of a long talk on   discernment that Benny and he must have. Proper and real reasons for becoming a priest were essential. Entering the priesthood was not like joining the Elks or the Boy Scouts. There was a long haul involved and no quitting – at least that was the hope " no quitting." They could see the Hudson River from where they sat. Occasionally a freight train passed by on the opposite side of the river and they could hear its lonely whistle across the water. The ground was covered with brown pine needles and squirrels kept charging across it either burying nuts or gathering pine needles for their nests. Benny remembered a story he once heard about how dumb squirrels were because they couldn't remember where they buried half the nuts they stored for winter.

Benny was the first to talk, "It still kinda' scares me when I realize that you and I are the only people in this whole order.

"It scares me a little too, Benny. But we have to keep up a good front and you might be the start of something good."

"I don't getcha'."

Albert smiled gave a slight shrug and said," Maybe you will attract others."

Benny nodded, shrugged his shoulders, started playing with a pine needle – spinning it around in his hand, " Let me ask you, Albert, really what is a priest? I mean all my life I've seen priests and all my life they've seemed different. I mean kind of special – set off – not like the ordinary Joes. I mean a priest comes into a room everybody stiffens – no more curse words – every sentence ending with 'Father ' this or 'Father' that – if he's special like that – how the hell do I get like that. I'm the son of a plumber from Queens and a lousy third class actuarian for a mammoth insurance company. Do I got to start taking pills or somethin' like that.

"No pills or something like that, Benny." Albert shifted in his seat and smiled. "A priest is a person who is in love with God and likes to help other people come to know God. And he does this by leading them in certain rites, like the mass, listening to their problems, helping with their families, and a lot of other things. He tries to help people reach out to other people and keep peace with them. He always prays for people."

Benny shook his head, "I don't know."

"You're not going to be a priest overnight – if you decide 'yes' , you will be studying for at least six years. Learning about men and women who have become saints, how to make good decisions, know the difference between right and wrong, what it means to pray and how to pray. All the time working with people who share, for the most part, the same values as yourself."

"Do I leave here?"

"No, not right away. Maybe if I'm lucky, you'll stay with me for a year and then if you still want to go ahead I'll move you to another place which will a lot more like a regular school. You are going to take some courses from me. But I teach in a rather informal manner and you won't find it tough."

Benny was silent for a couple of minutes then he said, "I never seen so many trees." His head spun around as he tried to see the tops of all the pines. "Can we walk down to the river? It looks great."

"Sure, It's a steep climb down and a steeper one back up."

"Let's try it."

They walked for a bit – neither said anything. Benny was tempted to start a conversation about wine growing in New York State or the Canadian Football league anything at all just to talk. After what seemed like hours to Benny (In fact about five minutes) Albert found a bench with a view of the river and open to the sky. Benny had walked around the property many times but he had never found this bench. Albert sat and motioned for Benny to sit across from him on a stump.

* *

MANHATTAN

Dave still couldn't sleep. His career as an advertising executive was in jeopardy. His boss, Rex, had almost laughed when Dave told him he lost the account 'due to attrition' – he remarked "Davey, we got bigger fish to fry so just get that skillet hot again."

Dave was still trying to heat up the skillet to fry the bigger fish but he was 'shut down' inside. He had run a successful campaign but the patient died. It was weeks ago but he still felt responsible. No matter what he thought about frying fish – he couldn't get St. Sebastians off his mind. When things like this happened he retreated to Phyllis, his psychiatrist.

The small sign next to the door read "Phyllis Lamont, Psychiatrist, Spiritual readings on request." Dave rang the bell and walked in.

She always sat opposite Dave and just a little close. He was pouring his heart out to her and explaining the amount of impressions he delivered each month on the magazine ads for St. Sebastians. The neat drawing and photos he made to accompany the ad – he

23

pulled a colored brochure out of his pocket and gave it to her to examine.

She held it and turned over all the folds and smiled and exclaimed, "It's beautiful."

"I know it."

Phyllis was wonderful that way. Dave always came to her when he needed a little boost in his psyche. She poured him a cup of tea and explained that in no way should he blame the shortage of vocations to St. Sebastians on his campaign – it was a world-wide phenomena – guys were not joining the priesthood in droves.

"But why?" He wanted to know.

"I can't tell you, but maybe you should visit the Cardinal. Maybe he could help and if he agreed with me that it was not your fault then maybe you will come to realize this and relieve yourself of this 'great' burden."

"That makes sense. Maybe I'll do that."

She continued talking and he was hardly listening. His mind was drifting and he really wasn't there – then suddenly, he was back, She was saying how much she admired him and even though it was irregular with patients she wanted him to go on a date with her.

His eyes opened wide, "You what? I hardly know you – I mean you know me – but I don't know you."

"I can tell you. I can tell you anything you want to know.'

"I've only been here seven times."

"Nine."

Phyllis was dribbling on. She was practically a virgin at 29. Practically because the only time she had sex was with kids in high school and that seemed like a game and not the real thing. She always felt that she was really missing something by not attending a college like 'State' or a small 'nun' school, instead she had to go to Princeton. Her whole life was the fault of a 94 she got in a junior year Math test. Her grade was always 100 in all her courses and her father almost killed her when she came home with a 94. He blamed it on the fact that she had stayed late in school with a boy – Harold. Harold was a first class nerd but he put his hand on her thigh when he was studying with her. She actually liked it a little and then his hand started creeping up her leg. She wasn't sure how far he would go but she was ready to go all the way - the lights blinked and the library closed. Her father made her feel like a jerk and she agreed not to stay after school with Harold or any other boy again.

All the way through college no other guy put his hand on her thigh like Harold. She spent all her time studying and still getting nothing but A's and no kisses. She couldn't understand it. Then when she moved to New York – she was afraid and stayed in her apartment most of the time – but she could talk a great game to her patients. They loved her because most of their problems were somehow related to sex and she always took the position they should get as much sex as possible. Yet she never had it.

Now sitting across from her was a handsome man, well-built, good character, her father was dead, she could take it no longer. She jumped up - "I want you..." She was on top of him. She threw her arms around him and began kissing him all over his face she squeezed him until it hurt. "Ever since I first saw you I have been excited by your face and body. I give you an appointment with no notice at all – it usually takes three weeks to make an appointment with me – but for you - the day you call is the day you got it."

"I know – I always thought business was slow..."

She cut him off with a kiss that reached to his stomach – "You can have me for anything..."

He was trying to wiggle from under the barrage of hands and kisses – "this is very nice but ..."

"All the sessions will be free...."

25

"Yes but I have to go right now...I promise I'll be back" He stood up and she fell to the floor – her dress was almost off (she had been trying to take it off on top of him) – He walked to the door, turned and said, " I am going, as you suggested, to see the Cardinal." He walked out.

* *

SO-HO

Baby was David's girl friend and confidant. She lived with David and she spent most of the day sprawled out on the big king size bed that dominated David's four room apartment. She was certainly a looker whom David had saved from the life of a hooker. David supported her and paid her a small stipend. She was still a hooker but the 'live in' kind. She was always after more money than the stipend but David managed to keep it under some kind of control.

David loved Baby when they were making love but when she wasn't performing, (and she could really perform) he tried to tell himself that someplace there was something better for him. At least he thought there was something better for him when he pictured himself as a rising young AD exec before the St. Sebastians thing made him doubt himself.

Phyllis, the psychiatrist, had acted crazy he thought. Did she want to really have sex right there in the room where she listened to his woes. That whole scene was crazy. He thought she was nice but that's about it 'nice.' Of course maybe he could go back and tell her that he would love to go out with her – and if he did there was no telling what might happen.

"Did you bring the Chinese?"

"Yes, I brought it." He always brought Chinese home for Baby on Wednesday nights. The same thing all the time 'moo shu pork and three egg rolls for Baby and vegetable chop suey for himself. Every Wednesday night they ate it in bed watched some guys play poker on TV and then make love and fall asleep. They watched poker because Baby liked to hear about the money being made... ."I'll raise you $250,000 – I'm all in for a $1,000,000 – David was sure they weren't really betting that much money but maybe they were and as far as Baby was concerned it was what they said it was. She knew nothing about Poker.

They moved into eating positions in the bed and began clicking chop sticks. David looked at Baby as she gulped her food and told him how good it was and how she almost died of starvation waiting for it. David smiled, but he was depressed. His career was not on track since St. Sebastians. He had no one to talk to about it. He would love to have a compassionate wife sitting with him instead of a sex machine. He knew lots of guys who would trade a wife for Baby in a New York minute but he was stuck with her.

Rice was coming out of the side of her mouth, "It's good, Honey, eat your chop suey."

He just kept staring at his food and not moving to take any.

"What's the matter Sweetie?"

David sighed, "You think I'm good at advertising don't you?"

"The best." She stopped for a second looked at him "What do you do - advertise? What's that?"

"I try to make people buy something or go someplace special. I prepared a lot of neat stuff trying to get young men to join this order of St. Sebastians and nobody joined."

Her head started nodding as if she understood.

"But I have failed. Something I advertised did not work. It did not work when I was sure it would. A whole seminary is going to close because of me. And now there is just one priest left and nobody with him.

"A seminary?"

"Place where men study to become priests its called St. Sebastians."

"I had no idea you were into religion."

"I'm not into religion – I try to get young men to join."

As he began to put away the paper dishes their food came in he continued to talk. He told her that the seminary had only one guy left and when he closed it – that was the end.

"What happens to the building and everything."

"If he's the last one then he sells it and disposes of the money. It all belongs to the last guy."

The dishes were in the trash and he had his clothes off to watch poker.

"Where is this place."

"Upstate – it's called St. Sebastians."

"Look honey" pointing to the guy with the purple vest on the TV, " he just went all in for 1 and a half million....doesn't that give you goose bumps?"

"Sure, Baby, but I'm tired." He turned over and thought about Phyllis the psychiatrist and the Cardinal and Father Albert. He was going to see the Cardinal and show him the campaign which should have gotten potential priests to visit St. Sebastians.

He thought that maybe it would not be a bad idea to personally visit St. Sebastian.

* *

The next morning Dave had his secretary call the Cardinal's office to make an appointment. She came back to him later in the day and informed Dave he would have to submit in duplicate the reasons for his requesting a visit. Dave spent the rest of the day working on the written request for the Cardinal. The next day it would go by messenger to his office. What the message said essentially was "I would like to talk to you about an advertising campaign."

"Make sure it goes on the good Agency Stationery, Maebelle, I want to impress the man."

* *

SO HO

Baby was still in bed when the downstairs bell rang, She pushed herself up on arm and hit the intercom, "Who is it?"

"Your brother, Marko."

"C'mon up."

Marko had to stop by and visit Baby every few days so he could give a report on 'anything new' for their mother. Their mother thought that Baby was working on a big New York Advertising Agency which, in Marko's opinion, was another way of saying what she did for a living.

"So how's Ma?"

Marko always felt uncomfortable with Baby, even though she was his sister, cuz she always spoke to him from a reclining position on the bed and she was hardly ever dressed in anything other than a loose nightgown.

"Ma is fine and she wants to know if you're eating OK."

"Tell her I'm just doing fine – real fine."

"No problems with David the Schmuck."

"He's not a schmuck. He works for a living. You are the schmuck."

"If not working makes you a schmuck then you and I..."

"I work for my living – its not easy rubbing David's feet every night and letting him have his way."

"Have his way? Ha! How lovely you put things being his little sex machine."

"He treats me good. I listen to his complaints. Last night a bunch of stuff about a place upstate that needs priests to join."

"He's not going to join is he?"

"No way." She slipped out of bed and walked into the Bathroom, "I gotta' change. He doesn't like to come home and see me still in my nighties at lunch time."

Marko walked around the small apartment. Why he stopped here he didn't know...except he needed $50.00. and she was his best bet.

From inside the bathroom she called out, "He was telling me last night that with just one priest – it's real bad...except that if he closes the place he is in charge of selling everything – how much ya want?"

"All I need is fifty. We got a big one coming up this week and I need a few bucks walking around money."

She came out of the bathroom dressed in a neat pair of blue slacks and a yellow turtleneck. "You know this is not a bank I got here – you oughta' get a steady job this 'airport business' of yours is not too regular and I don't think legal."

"All I do is drive a truck."

"Where you drive it is the problem?" She went into the kitchen area and called him, "Stay there and keep your eyes closed." She opened the refrigerator door and took fifty dollars out of the cheese drawer. She came back in and handed him the fifty, "I expect it back."

Marko took the ' cold' fifty, and said, "No problem - right after the airport job." Blew her a kiss and left.

* *

QUEENS

Benny's big brother, MO, the plumber, being a loyal and faithful member of the plumbers union attended the wake of Zippy a good union man for more than sixty years. Zippy's real name was Phil Zipparo, and the wake was in the neighborhood on 218th street.

When MO arrived at the wake, Dutch, head of the locals meets him at the door and tells him. "You got to be an honor guard."

"A what?" said MO.

"Stand beside the coffin to show respect and honor to 'ole Zippy. Goldie is doing it and I need two people."

"Why me? I didn't know Zippy that good."

"You – because you and Goldie were the only two guys that wore ties to this affair. You just have to stand there."

MO nodded to Goldie and took his place at the other end of the casket. He glanced down at Zippy and thought to himself – "Holy Shit I didn't think that was Zippy I always thought Zippy was ..."and he spotted the guy sitting down who he always thought was Zippy. "I feel weird. Come to see one guy and it's another. I wonder who that guy sitting is- he's not Zippy. Jeez what a mess."

He looked over at Goldie and nodded to him – he nodded back.

The lady greeting everybody must be Zippy's wife – she bowed her head to MO and slowly walked towards him...

"It's so nice of you to be standing in honor of Phil. He always thought you were the best plumber in the whole union."

MO smiled and nodded "Thank you. Phil, we always called him, Zippy, he was a really great guy."

MO was sure that lying here in a funeral home was not really lying – it was comforting. He had been listening to the praises of

31

Zippy and if he were half of what people were saying in praise of him, his death would be declared a national holiday.

Zippy's wife reached out and took his hand, " if only Zippy waited a while longer to die then your brother could say the mass. It is such a wonder he is becoming a priest."

* *

After the wake closed, Goldie and MO, with their ties still on, walked over to The Joint for a few beers. They sat down and ordered two.

" MO, Your little brother is becoming a priest?"

" Yeah – he's trying it. I don't know how long he'll last."

" Is it true they don't get married?"

"That's true."

"But they still have sex, right?"

"No way, Goldie, that's bad – "

"Jeez, that must be rough."

"Like anything else – you get used to it."

Goldie sipped his beer and was silent, " You get used to no sex. I suppose it's possible."

" Benny can handle that part – I think."

" Good for Benny." Another period silence as Goldie stared at whiskies displayed on the back of the bar, " Where is he?"

"Upstate. A place called St Sebastians."

"Never heard of it. But I ain't heard about a lot of churches."

"It's not exactly a church, Goldie, it's the kind of place where some priests teach other guys to become priests."

"Kinda' like a priest college and holy too, with a lot of priests hanging around."

Well, they don't have many priests – as a matter of fact they only have one plus Benny.

" Wow! That's dangerous or somethin'."

" If the priest dies – Benny is the only member left and Benny tells me he has to take over running the whole place."

"You mean the last guy standing gets the whole place."

"And Benny tells me it's beautiful - acres and acres of land and buildings as big as Madison Square Garden."

"So Benny lives and he wins the works."

"Yeah, but I'm sure that's not his plan."

"Wow – what a set-up."

"One more beer and talk to me about the Mets...."

ST. SEBASTIANS

Benny and Albert were sitting in the chapel.

" You're saying, Albert, that all great religions have had a prophet not just the Catholic?"

"Well, Moses was the prophet for the Jewish people. Today many Jews look upon Moses as their great Biblical leader. Then of course Mohammed came to the people of the East and the Muslim religion grew. Christ came to the Jewish people and was trying to change their thinking into something more in the spirit. All the Protestant religions are Christian, and more or less, off shoots of the first Christian religion. That is the religion we have. Other Eastern religions came along Buddhism, and Hinduism and they prospered."

"Are they all bad?"

"Not at all. All religions teach God, in some form, and believe in him or her, the same as we believe in God. It's the same God, but thousands of way of looking at him or her."

"That's not what Father Finnegan says."

"There's nothing bad about what Father Finnegan teaches it's just not the way the Church feels today. And really it's not what the church ever taught. Father Finnegan just comes from a different time and place."

"Then it's okay what Father Finnegan teaches."

"Correct, he's not all wrong, but today our religion feels that all people, from Eskimos to children in the deepest Congo, are children of God. Some people call him Allah, some Buddha, some other things."

"But it's the same God."

"Exactly. The only thing that is really important for all people is to - Love God and Love your neighbor. And everyone in the world is really our neighbor."

Benny sat for a time and was deep in thought. Albert was telling him that he had to love everybody, even Grunwald his ex-boss in the insurance company. Grunwald was close to a monster the way he pinched asses of all the girls and made us all pinch pennies and docked Smitty his pay when he had to rush home cause his kid was hit by a car. And the time...well, I have to stop thinking about him and I have to learn to love him. That's a pretty big order. But Albert was pushing the envelope a little and really trying to make him realize some of the deep stuff he was getting into.

Benny had been at St Sebastian's for almost several weeks now and every day Albert and he would sit and talk. They really didn't have a class as such but the whole time he was with Albert he was learning.

Albert told him the best thing he liked about being a priest is that he learned to move inside his head (that's the way Albert put it) to a better place. He was able to take 'time out' from the monotony of living and think on himself and relax. He called the relaxing "bein' in the lap of God" but Benny was a far, far, way from doing that. When he relaxed he either fell asleep or started wondering what was going on in Queens - Benny could not yet see Queens as the lap of God.

He and Albert shared cooking and Benny was learning to cook pretty good. He could now make Spaghetti in meat sauce (his meat balls always fell apart), a decent omelet, salad, cut up a chicken. He hadn't actually cooked a chicken yet be was sure he could do it. He always made a simple sandwich and a can of soup for lunch. Albert even shared doing the dishes and cleaning up with Benny. Once a week they would go out together for a pizza and a few beers.

Benny got up everyday at 5:30 and served as an altar boy at Albert's 6 o'clock Mass. Benny kinda' liked the Mass. Just he and Albert and Albert told stories with some kind of moral included and explained the readings. Benny got to know lots of little duties he had to perform as an Altar boy. He never knew it when he served Mass for Father Finnegan while in grade school that he was really an Acolyte. Acolyte was one of the first steps in becoming a priest.

After their simple breakfast they would work around the property always finding something to do

Benny had never weeded a garden before. He couldn't really tell the difference between a weed and a flower. He watched Albert carefully and followed his lead on which was which. But more than weed the garden Albert would talk to him about peace and care for the things that grow. Benny thought that beans and tomatoes and all vegetables got to Queens by some kind of magic. But here he watched and learned as he observed Albert work to clear away debris and give the vegetables a chance to grow. Albert would talk to him of the work of God happening in the soil and how we have a certain obligation to take care of the soil and the plants. He referred once as the weeds as things that try to keep the good things from growing just "like us we have plenty of things in our lives that keep us from growing."

Benny thought about this the rest of the day and into the night.

* *

KENNEDY AIRPORT

Baby's brother Marko was sitting in a truck alongside a wire fence that surrounded the freight terminal at JFK airport. He and Felix, his partner, had just cut a hole about 4' by 4' in the fence and Felix had slipped inside. Marko got paid $500 for the nights work – this was 10 times or more what he got paid working in his regular job at "Honey Hots" the fast food place on Jamaica Avenue. All he had to really do was wear gloves and not get fingerprints on Leo's truck. This he did religiously.

He was thinking about his sister Baby and how she socked that guy for a bundle every week and she didn't do anything but what she did natural. If their mother ever found out about this there would be screaming and shouting and fighting all over the place. Of course his mother was always pissed at him for selling hamburgers – she didn't know about his airport work.

"Where the hell is Felix – he should be back by now" – he never knew where Felix went or what he did and he wasn't about to ask. All he knew is that Felix would go through the hole in the fence and about 30 minutes later return with a bunch of guys carrying boxes. The boxes went in the truck and then he and Felix would drive it to a street in Brooklyn – they stopped at this address and guys poured out of a brownstone and emptied the truck in about two minutes. After the truck was empty they brought it back to Leo. Easy and simple and he collected $500. "Where the hell is Felix?"

Marko heard a siren and two police cars came by really fast. "Somebody has got a problem."

The door opposite the driver opened and Felix jumped in, "Drive – get out of here – but not too fast."

"What happened, Felix? You look rattled!"

"Rattled? Drive! Get us out of here. We've been made. Some guy was waiting when we moved in on the shipment."

"We been stealing all this time."

"Of course, you think you get 5 long ones for picking up my aunt Pixie's luggage."

"What do we steal?"

"Everything we can."

Marko started driving. "Felix, if we are trying flee from the cops they will have all the exits covered."

"Shit – you're right."

Marko kept driving then he had an idea, "Felix, I got an idea."

Felix looked at him and shook his head, "You are not an 'idea' man, Marko, – I'm not sure I'll like your idea."

"Listen, I say we leave the truck - go into one of the terminals and stay there a few days."

"Stay in a terminal?"

"Yeah, they got bathrooms and comfortable chairs and I saw a movie where a guy stayed in a terminal for a whole year."

"It's an idea – it really is – let's do it."

Marko pulled over and stopped the truck in a 'no parking' zone and said, "Let's get out – we can make it to the Continental terminal from here."

They both jumped out and started walking casually through a field to the Continental terminal. Marko was the first to speak, "Do you think Big Leo will be mad at us for leaving the truck?"

* *

Albert and Benny were walking in the gardens. Albert stopped. "Benny, you have been here almost a few months and, in my opinion you are doing OK."

Benny nodded, "Sure, Albert, I'm OK. Some of the books you gave me to read are a little rough but I'm beginning to understand them. The one about 'Introduction to Divine Life' was good. I am re-reading parts of that one."

"That's a good idea."

"It's so quiet up here with nothing to disturb us that reading is easy."

Albert stopped walking and pointed to a bench. "Let's stop a few minutes. I want to show you something."

From a box he was carrying he removed a Franciscan robe. "Benny this is for you. I have walked with you enough and talked with you enough to make me believe that you really want to become a member of Saint Sebastian. This is the robe we wear. We are an off-shoot of the Franciscans and we honor that and hold that dear. I wear this robe and you may wear it."

Benny was quiet he took the robe gently and held it , then he looked at Albert. "Is it really alright."

"Yes."

"You probably know about St. Francis and this robe is modeled after what he chose to wear – when he decided to put on clothes."

"What do you mean?"

"Ahh," Albert leaned back his voice was quizzical, "You don't know the story of Francis."

"Not really."

"Well, Francis was a kind of playboy back in Assisi, Italy, eight hundred years ago. He stayed out late and slept late until one day he saw a poor beggar asking for help. Francis was transfixed. He got down from his horse and gave the beggar his clothes and there before all the villagers - he stood naked. He spent the rest of his life working with the poor and oppressed and moving daily closer and closer to a union with God."

"He gave up everything."

"Everything. Even the clothes he was wearing."

Benny was quiet he fingered the robe Albert had given him – then he stood and not saying a word he slipped it over his shoulders and let it fall to the ground. Benny looked down at the robe and quietly spoke, "How could he give up everything?"

"He really wanted to help people and he loved God. In a sense you have given up everything to be here – and I pray everyday that you will stay here."

Benny kept nodding is head.

Albert said, "Come for a walk with me

" But, Benny, there is a little problem I have. For the past year I have had scheduled a retreat..."

"Retreat, what's that?"

" It is a retreat a 'going away from everyday activities to a quiet place to pray and get closer to God. I go to a monastery near Saranac Lake for 15 days with other priests, who are retreat masters, men who help you in prayer."

"You are going away." \

"Just for fifteen days."

"And I will be alone..."

"Unfortunately, but you have nothing to fear. You can handle it – I am sure. Before you came, I would simply lock the doors and go off, but since you are here I can leave our doors open."

Two days later Albert left for his retreat and Benny was in charge of the empty building and everything that went with it.

* *

THE CARDINAL'S OFFICE

Dave's secretary had made an appointment with the Cardinal for 2 O'clock. He was advised not to be late since his Excellency kept a very busy and disciplined schedule.

At fifteen minutes before 2 Dave was sitting in the parlor outside his 'Excellencies' office. Dave was happy that the monsignor who had replied to him had used the term Excellency when referring to the cardinal because he had forgotten what he was called and Dave did not want to goof on any protocol. He had his complete advertising plan of St. Sebastian with him and he felt confidant that he could make a good case for continuing with the campaign.

The room smelled a little like a church and Dave decided the smell was good and he would make an effort to attend church on a more regular basis. He remembered when He went about four years ago everything seemed to have changed from his boyhood. The service was shorter and the homily was much more complicated than he remembered them being. The priest wore sneakers which came as a bit of cultural shock to Dave. He supposed that he was either on his way to play tennis or he was having trouble with his feet. Dave sat in the church and created the scenario of sore feet for the priest and therefore wearing the sneakers was a forgivable offense.

Dave got up and felt the walls. He thought from his seat that they were covered with upholstery and he was right. They were probably easier to take care of – just vacuum them occasionally and never have to paint. Good idea!

The door opened and a priest spoke, "Mr. David Fields?"

"Yes."

"Come with me."

He followed the priest through the door. Seated at the far end of the room behind a large mahogany desk was a perfectly groomed gray-haired man. The priest led him to a chair off to the right of the desk and gestured for him to sit. He felt he was in a throne room and the king was about to behead him. He looked around the room while the Cardinal shuffled through some papers. One wall was covered with framed awards, degrees, and celebrities' signed pictures. He thought to himself that signed picture of Lou Gherig would probably bring 5 grand on E-Bay and the one of Mickey Mantle at least as much. He thought 'gosh, he's even got Marilyn Monroe', on his wall.

A voice startled him, " Admiring my collection."

"It's great and must be worth a fortune."

"It belongs to the church. They were here when I got here."

"Oh, that's nice."

"I understand you're from the Whippet Advertising agency, How can I help you?"

His voice had the ring of authority in it that Dave always sensed when talking to any client. They always have the feel and timbre in their voice of knowing what the last words of any discussion will be before the discussion has taken place. He had hoped this would be different.

Dave, his voice in the best form he could muster, began, " I represented St. Sebastian's for several years in their campaign to bring priests into their order."

The Cardinal raised his right hand and beckoned with a finger to the priest sitting opposite Dave. The priest arose and crossed to the Cardinal...

"Shall I wait?, Dave asked a little gingerly.

The Cardinal was blunt, "No - Keep talking."

As Dave talked about the campaign, the priest whispered in the Cardinal's ear. The Cardinal nodded and the priest left the room.

Dave had his display ads spread over the Cardinal's desk. "As you can see from these ads that we were directing the campaign to the heart of the 20 to 40 year old group, They were placed in media with a readership in the millions..."

The priest returned and placed a note in the Cardinal's hand...

"Shall I wait?"

"No, please continue, " the Cardinal shot back, but his eyes were on the note he had been given and not on the display ads.

Dave assured the Cardinal that a campaign such as this would be up to 90% effective in achieving the goal. He presented the cardinal with a graph demonstrating the success in a Boy Scout Campaign, a Girl Scout Campaign, a camp for clowns, two successive campaigns for improving the enrollment in a Hockey camp. The figures were impressive and Dave droned on.

The Cardinal called the Monsignor over again and again the monsignor left the room and came back this time with a manila folder for the Cardinal.

Dave finished with, "I believe your highness...

The monsignor piped up..."Excellency."

Dave turned a little red..."Oh excuse me your Excellency, I didn't mean Highness."

The Cardinal nodded, "You're forgiven."

Dave nodded his head several times, he wondered if the Cardinal wouldn't really rather be 'Highness' but more than that he wondered if the Cardinal had heard anything he said – that monsignor kept running in and out...he continued, "I believe your excellency, the figures speak for themselves. Our agency has run many campaigns with stellar results and if we could just be given another chance at Saint Sebastian, we could...easily up the enrollment at that fine institution with figures that would make you proud."

Dave sat down.

The Monsignor crossed his legs.

The Cardinal leaned back and looked at Dave.

There was silence. Thirty seconds passed – more silence.

The Cardinal looked Dave squarely in the eye – more silence.

Finally the Monsignor spoke, "Are you finished? Do you have anything more to say?"

"No, I just wondered if , perhaps, you would like to look at the graphs again that demonstrate our success."

The Cardinal said, "Thank you Mr..." and he glanced down at the business card Dave had given to the secretary..."Mr. Fields, I believe we have seen and heard all that is necessary."

The monsignor piped up. "We will be in touch Mr. Fields " pause of ten seconds while Dave stared at him, "when we feel in need of your services. Thank you very much for coming."

He rose and pointed to the door and waited for Dave to walk with him.

At the door Dave turned to the Cardinal, "Good meeting you, maybe we could do lunch sometime."

"Mr. Fields, Please," And the door opened and shut as Dave a bit groggy and shaky got in the Elevator and went down.

The Monsignor returned to the Cardinal.

The Cardinal spoke first, "What the hell was that all about? I was told his agency was prepared to be a major benefactor not do whatever he was doing. And where in God's Holy Name is this Saint Sebastian place I never heard of it."

"There is mention of it in the Manila folder. Page forty-three, there's a list its two up from the bottom."

The Cardinal looked on page forty-three, "they do have a lot of land. Look into it, Harold, and maybe we'll visit it someday."

* *

KENNEDY AIRPORT

"Felix, we have been living here for three days don't ya' thank we should move on?

"Are you complaining Marko. We have heat and nice bathrooms and it's really not too bad sleeping here. We can't leave yet – we take our orders from Leo."

"Have you told Leo of our dilemma?"

"Not yet."

"I think Leo is going to be wondering about his truck – we just left it and ran."

"They were about to shoot us."

They both slouched forward in the waiting room chairs of Continental Gate 37 and closed their eyes.

Felix spoke again, "let us wait another day or so before I call Leo. It will probably be a difficult discussion."

"And ask him if he can bring us underwear."

I ain't gonna' ask him for anything. I imagine he's gonna' be too pissed off to listen and if he comes lookin' for us he might shoot us.

Marko grumbled a soft Okay. They were quiet for a few minutes then Marko spoke, "I think I'm having triple burger at Wendy's tonight without the cheese."

* *

ST. SEBASTIANS

MO decided it was time he put his little brother Benny to a test. If he really liked the place – he was going to leave him alone but if he had any doubts then Mo was going to get Benny the hell outa' there. He followed Benny's directions and drove up to the entrance to Saint Sebastian. He got out and went to the front door. He knocked and banged on the huge oak door – but no answer. He walked around the side of the building and there was a guy – dressed like a monk – pulling weeds out of a flower bed. "Excuse me, guy, can you tell me..."

The guy looked up then half ran toward him, "MO, how the heck ya' been?"

"What happened to your hair and where did you get that robe?"

"The clothes are regular issue and I cut my hair – no big deal. But how the heck are you? You look a little pale?"

"I'm fine." They hugged.

Benny took MO on a tour of the grounds. He showed him all the flower beds - the walking trails that wound around and through the trees. He showed him a small Pond full of Frogs but few fish. He brought him inside the main building and showed him his room. There wasn't much in it "but it's all mine."

Benny and MO made themselves a dinner of pasta, "one of the things I can cook." Benny explained that he and Albert, the priest in charge, and my boss, had to do their own cooking. "Someday Albert hopes to get a cook." After dinner they talked about the neighborhood and growing up there.

"I never thought I could ever come to a place like this. I used to take money from the box where people lit candles. Sometimes I'd get four quarters and my conscience bothered me so whenever I took a quarter I'd blow out a candle – I didn't want the candle burning for nothing."

MO almost yelled at him for taking the money, "Did you know that Sister Immaculate always screamed at me cause' she was sure I was taking it. And all the time it was my little brother."

"Remember the time there was a hole in the roof and the priest didn't notice it during the mass for the kids...but all the kids giggled at it and he thought they were giggling at him. I know who made the hole."

"Who was it."

"Andy Fotana. He was in the church with me late at night and we were up in the balcony and he found a door that opened up to the plaster ceiling of the church. He started walking across one of the beams that held the plaster and he fell. Man that was one lucky Fotana who started to fall into the church – but he grabbed a beam and held on. I had to crawl in after him and pull him up through the hole."

"What did Father Finnegan say?"

"We never told him. I think he felt it just fell."

The two of them laughed as they visualized Andy Fotana hanging over the church.

"One thing I know for sure is that Andy prayed that night in church."

MO talked about how hard it was to teach Benny to ride a bike " you must have fallen down fifty times in one block. I thought you'd kill yourself."

Benny talked about Billie Atwater, the girl in his seventh grade class, he was convinced that he was in love with her and they would be married and live in Manhattan, "Where is she now, Mo?"

"I heard about her the other day, she's got two kids and divorced, but she's still pretty."

"Man, that's sad."

"That's the way it is in our world – lots of things happen that you can't believe. It's a regular zoo out there."

"MO, do you think it's worse now than when we were growing up.?"

"It seems that way."

"I don't think it's too different. It's just that when we were kids our parents kept a lot of things hidden from us by not talking about them. The world really doesn't change much and people didn't either."

"Drugs, Benny, drugs make us different."

Benny was quiet. He sat in silence with his brother for almost a minute. He stood up. He spoke, "yeah, I know." He turned and left.

MO followed him to the room Benny had given him.

* *

At seven in the morning MO got up. Everything was silent. He got dressed and sneaked down to the kitchen. Benny was already there eating a bowl of oatmeal and drinking coffee. "Man, Benny, you get up early. I thought I was the first one."

"I get up at 5 everyday." He smiled at MO's reaction. "I'm becoming a changed man in all ways."

"I can't believe it."

"Have some cereal and coffee."

MO sat down and ate. After his breakfast Mo wanted a shower and Benny directed him to one and gave him a towel and soap.

"I'll be waiting outside, MO. Take your time. I'll see you in a while."

MO finished up and felt better. He came down to the kitchen. The dishes were done. He walked outside and saw Benny sitting on a slight rise watching the river . He watched him for about five minutes and he hardly moved. He wondered what he was doing and he walked to him. "What's doing, Benny?"

Benny turned to MO, "I was praying."

"Praying?"

Benny asked MO to sit next to him. He explained that most of the praying he was learning to do at Saint Sebastian was not saying the Our Father and Hail Mary. It was more just taking time and imaging God with you. Benny said he thought about the hills, river, and trees as some of the things that God gave him. He told Mo that you had to learn what you felt towards God and then prayer came easier. It was not like Father Finnegan used to say that unless you say Our Fathers and Hail Marys you would surely burn. "But don't get me wrong about Our Fathers and Hail Marys they are wonderful prayers and I pray them a lot but talking to God as a loving father is much more effective for me."

MO shook his head, "I don't know."

"Listen, MO, what's right for you is right for you. I'm just saying there are different ways."

The rest of the day MO and Benny walked around the grounds, weeded gardens, cleaned bathrooms, put out garbage, and Mo fixed three dripping faucets.

That night they went out for Pizza.

In the morning MO had a cup of coffee and went outside to the same spot he had met him yesterday.

"More prayers?'

Benny looked up and smiled at his big brother, "That's right – more prayers – more every day."

"Benny, I been thinking. Last night when I didn't fall asleep right away, I did some thinking and I haven't done much of that in months."

Benny smiled, " that's good."

"But the thinking was about you – and what you're doing."

"I'm happy, MO."

I know you are now, but have you looked at the way things work for you in the future. I mean you get along great here - nothing to worry about –meals – bed – great scenery. Can it last forever? Your buddy Albert can't keep this place open forever – I mean, Benny, there are no other guys except you and him. I don't know much about the economics of running a place this big but it has to cost a fortune. You're going to have to move and who knows what the next place will be like. You can't be married – have a family – no kids – it will be a lonely life."

"I can love your kids."

"I don't have any."

"But you will. Won't you?"

"After I marry I suppose I will."

Benny got up and walked a few steps toward the river, then he turned and looked at MO for a few seconds before he spoke softly to MO. "I suppose you will and I hope you'll be very happy. I am happy here. It's a funny thing, MO, when you get into the...I guess the, swing, of praying, it feels good. I'm not lonely when I pray. I'm not lonely when I work in the gardens around here. I'm not lonely when I do things that make it easier for Albert and I to function. I'm not lonely when Albert says Mass.

When I read that ad that told me about this place – I figured ' what the hell' it said to give it as try so I did. I was serious about finding a place to do things outside an office – I was hoping this was it. And you know what MO, this is it."

"I'll see ya', Benny," he walked to his car, turned once and said he'd be back.

Benny watched him go and realized how much he really did miss his family and the 'hood' but knew he would not go back there to live.

* *

QUEENS

Goldie worked with Irish for a man named Angel who conducted a neighborhood collection agency. Angel had requested their presence in his offices for a business discussion.

They were sitting on orange crates outside the door leading to Mr. Angel's office. They shifted and were very uncomfortable.

"Goldie , I don't understand why Mr. Angel doesn't have chairs out here."

"Ours not reason how or why – just do or die. "

"Please don't use the word 'die' it makes me very nervous, Goldie."

"Relax, Irish, relax – sing to yourself."

"Sing to myself? I am not sure I know how...Mr. Angel has never had us in for a business discussion before."

"Irish, maybe he has a promotion in mind for us."

"That would be very nice."

"On the other hand, Irish, he may be upset over some recent failings we have had."

"That would be very bad."

The door opened and an immense man beckoned to them to follow him. He leads them into an office that is much nicer than the orange crate waiting room.

The immense man gestures for them to sit, "Mr. Angel will be with you shortly."

Goldie and Irish take a seat. Irish squirms in his seat and says, " I always thought Angel was Angel's first name."

Goldie looks at him, " It is."

"Then how come the giant referred to him as Mr. Angel. I ain't Mr. Irish, I am plain Irish, if you want to be formal you call me Mr. Downey, not Mr. Irish."

"I never knew you had a last name."

"Sure, I do.."

"Well, if I ever want to get formal I know what to do, Mr. Downey."

A side door opened and the giant held it open while Angel walked in. He was about three feet shorter and about four times rounder than the man who showed them in. He sat down at the big desk. Goldie figured the chair must be on a platform cause Angel looked very tall behind the desk. He was now looking way down at Goldie and Irish.

"Nice to see you, boys."

They both muttered a 'nice to see ya' back.

Angel reached in his desk drawer and pulled out a long knife. Irish squirmed and Goldie gulped – then an almost audible sigh of relief as he started cutting up a peach. "I used to smoke cigars but I had to give them up for my throat. Want a peach? Harold get the boys a...."

The giant moved but Goldie and Irish both said "no thanks, Mr. Angel."

Irish and Goldie watched wide- eyed as Mr. Angel pealed all the skin off peach – he had a continuous ring of skin curling around on the desk. The whole action took about five minutes. Finally Mr. Angel finished and Irish said, "Nice job – you did the whole thing in one slice."

"It's a challenge and now Goldie and Irish, I would like to talk to you about the challenge in your jobs – you are not doing so nice. As a matter of fact you are not accepting the challenge and you are doing lousy."

Goldie, with a tremor in his voice, spoke, "What do you mean, Mr. Angel. We are working very hard. All our clients are very diligent and make payments right on time."

"Goldie, the bottom line is getting out of hand. I am going to require you to meet the bottom line figure which I am going to raise."

Irish looked a little pale as he spoke, "Geez, Mr. Angel, we cannot raise the tariff, we are already knocking off almost 10% of gross receipts."

"They're all little guys – they can't give much more and meet their rent," Goldie leaned forward as he spoke, "you wouldn't want to hurt anybody – would you?"

"Goldie, I hope it's not surprising to you that I had to hurt some people to get behind this desk."

Goldie and Irish leaned back and glanced at each other and shrugged their shoulders with a 'what's gonna' happen' look.

Mr. Angel bit into the juicy peach and some juice squirted across the room and hit Irish in the eye. He grabbed his eye and held it.

"I am sorry, Irish, but the peach is a little juicy."

"That's the way I like them," offered Goldie.

There was a lull as they watched Mr. Angel eat the peach – he took a nice bite out of it then slobbered out a question, "You boys got any ideas."

"About What?" asked Irish.

"Improving the bottom line. You don't want to raise the rate of pay-off so give me another idea. I am reasonable."

"Do you need anybody shot or hit very hard in the knees."

"Not at the present. But if your collections do not improve I might need someone. This peach was so good it made me feel good enough to give you 48 hours to up your collections – to the amount what I am accustomed to. Now go! "

Irish and Goldie started scurrying towards the door. Goldie stopped. He turned to Mr. Angel and said, "I have an idea."

Angel was leaving by another door and not paying attention to Goldie's words.

Goldie continued, "It could be worth as much as a million dollars."

Angel turned back from the door. "What did you say?"

Goldie walked back into the room.

Angel returned to his chair, "This better be good, Goldie, I am not in a good mood."

Goldie then explains in as much detail as he can the situation Mo had told him about after Zippy's wake. The place Benny had joined Saint Sebastian with no priests and the idea that the whole place could revert to the last priest who was member of the order. He explained that it was hundreds of acres – very big but no priests.

Angel listened carefully and said, "What is your plan?"

"Irish and I will join the Saint Sebastian and if necessary we will rid by force anybody left and we will get the whole place and naturally we will give it to you since you have been so good to us."

Angel was quiet. He thought about it for a long time. Finally he spoke, " I am going to have 'the book' look at this and I will let you know tomorrow – goodbye."

* *

KENNEDY AIRPORT

Back at the airport Felix gets off the phone with his contact. He has been told to lay low and hide for awhile in the meantime they can stay where they are. Felix tells Marko this news .

"You didn't speak to Big Leo?"

"Not yet. The truck might make him angry."

Marko is gulping down his third egg McMuffin., in between gulps, he said,"I remember a movie about a guy who just ate fast food for a month and he almost died.," he glanced at his partner Felix, "We got to stop this soon. I need some home made soup or a steak."

Felix reminds him that they take orders from somebody who is higher up and secondly they are still subject to incarceration by the authorities

Marko relates to Felix the perfect place to hide is this place upstate call St. Sebastians where they have this big house for priests and there are no priests!...maybe they could make like they are joining for a few weeks until Felix is able to reestablish his connections. Call the boss back and tell him about the place."

"Not yet - I will when we have protection from the church."

Marko mused about the word protection – "I suppose we do need that for a while."

They both finished their breakfast in silence. Then Felix stood up and said, "Let's get outa' here."

* *

ST. SEBASTIANS

Albert returned from his retreat and sat with Benny for talk sessions on what his duties would entail and what , hopefully, his life would become.

They were sitting at their favorite bench overlooking the river.

Albert sltarted talking "I want to talk to you about praying. I have been meaning to do this for sometime now and what I am going to say is just a kind of format or outline on which you can hang your prayer hat, but everybody really prays differently and all of us have our own way."

Benny nodded agreement.

"I hope what I am saying will be taken in the right light. I don't want you to change your prayer life – God knows that – it was strong prayer in some manner or fashion that brought you here. I believe that and I would never change that but I have noticed you sometimes watch me pray and I want to share what I go through.

Do you get me, Benny?"

"I get ya'."

"First find a place – like the place we are in now. I pray often from this spot and it has meaning to me. After you are comfortable, Close your eyes, think about the presence of God, and use word like these,

'Lord I believe you are present in me. At the center of me – I want to be just with you, and think 'Lord let me experience your presence and your love.' Then Choose a word or a name that has meaning for you and begin to recite the word over and over again. The repitition of the word will help keep distractions away...soon you can aware of the presence of the Lord and the word fades away...but when distractions come go back to the word and you can refocus on God

At the end of the prayer time – 10 to 20 minutes – thank God for his being and ask for his love to remain with you and then say the good old Our Father – just like your Father Finnegan taught you."

Benny listened to 'the lesson' and felt good about it. They were both relaxing and Benny decided to bring up a subject he had been avoiding.

"Albert, have you ever heard strange noises at night?"

"Like doors opening and closing or maybe tree limbs outside."

"No noises like somebody walking in the hallways or making noises in the kitchen – funny noises."

Albert gave a big sigh and shook his head as if he were trying to stop something from happening, "Benny, I have to tell you a story that goes way back. St. Sebastian's was originally owned by a Dutch family – the Huntsel family. They were fur trappers and food merchants before the Revolutionary War and they amassed an enormous fortune. In the middle of the nineteenth century they had lost most of the fortune. Trade along the Hudson River had slowed down considerably and the family, which had earlier converted to Catholicism, was dying off. Mr. Huntsel's family met with a tragic accident on a sleigh ride – the horse who was pulling the sled went over a cliff and they all died...except Mr. Huntsel who had been visiting New York."

Benny was intrigued by the story and wondered what this had to do with noises in the night. "I could see how the horses could go over the cliff in the snow...I almost fell the other day. The hill is pretty darn steep near the river."

"Mr. Huntsel was devastated he decided to give the property to the church. His closest contact with the church was his local pastor who accepted the generous offer. But the pastor's church had only 90 parishioners and the size of the house was 100 rooms. The pastor a man named Fr. Geralds, and his young assistant Fr. Michael, prayed over it and then moved into the main house but they decided to make it a community. Their 90 parishioners moved in and worked the land and raised food crops and started a dairy. Fr. Geralds wrote for other priests to join him and they did and other young men asked to join and that is how our order started."

"Pretty neat, but what about the noises"

"I'm getting to that – for about 100 years the new order at the House of St. Sebastian thrived. Then the bottom fell out. The original 90 and their offspring was gone and from a high of about 75 priests we kept dropping off to 'me' and now you."

"What happened to all the priests?"

"Most of them died and others left the church and others joined more successful orders. When they started leaving I started hearing noises like you hear. One night I stood in the hallway and shouted 'maker of the noises stop' and they did. And from the end of the hallway a guy appeared."

"Wow."

"The guy told me his name was Rodney. He said he was a ghost sent by his father, Bertram Huntsel, to insure that St. Sebastians stays open and does the work of the Church. In other words Rodney is like our guardian angel helping us keep open. But Rodney has got to come up with cash soon or he's going back to where he came from as a loser."

"You know I don't believe in ghosts."

"You will after you meet Rodney."

"Albert, are you telling me there is a ghost and I am going to meet him or it."

"Exactly."

"But, Albert, there is no such thing as ghosts."

"As Christians, we believe in an after-life and I think this 'ghost' kind of proves there is life after death." Albert then explained that death brings us to a spirit world and since ghosts are spirits it could be possible that spirits or ghosts can be active in our world. "I really don't know Benny, but I do know that Rodney is a real ghost – he has even argued with me."

"Argued with you about what?"

"That I have got to get more people to join our community. I explain that the world of future priests out there is shrinking fast – you know that. And you know there isn't anything I can do about it."

They started to leave. Albert explained that he should never worry about Rodney. He also said, " we started talking about prayer today and when I get back we'll talk about Sacraments and Mass and Saints."

"You have to go away again?"

"Do you miss me?"

"Well this is a pretty big operation for me to run by myself."

"You did great. I only have to go to Wappingers Falls a priest friend of mine needs an operation and it is custom there to have mass every day so he has asked me to come in. On the weekend he has other help so I'll be back Sunday and maybe I'll be able to stay here for a while. Besides you did great last time – I didn't see any problems.

They continued walking and talking to the kitchen.

* *

QUEENS

Mr. Angel has Goldie and Irish sitting before him. He is telling them of the great hurt they have caused him by neglecting to make their payments to him - and on time. He informs them that the usual punishment for such an action is some form of death - plain and simple - " you are no longer entitled to live." But, and this is their salvation, if they go to St. Sebastians and join the order and wait for the priest to have an untimely accident - he nods to the lawyer type, who nods back, then you guys will be the owners of the land since you will be the last surviving members of the order, Goldie reminds Angel that he is not even Catholic but Angel says you will be a "happy convert." Irish believes it .

"Leave immediately and let me know when the 'demise' has taken place."

* *

MANHATTAN

Marko and Felix took a bus into the city from the airport. They were careful to act normal and not arouse any suspicion of who they were or what they had done at JFK. Twice Marko was sure they were being followed by a lady. Marko kept running ahead and turning a corner to wait if the lady tail was still following Felix – twice he was disappointed that they were in the clear.

"Maybe this means we're free Felix. Nobody cares what we did and maybe we can go home."

"What it means, Marko, is that Big Leo cares unless he had had a very severe memory loss – which I doubt."

"I almost forgot about him."

"Not a good idea."

When they reached the city, Marko called Baby and got the location of Benny's 'priest place.' He then hit her up for a hundred bucks which she reluctantly gave him with the admonishment – " you should get a real job – I have to work for my money, you should learn to do it." He took the money and told her he'd like to do 'learn to do it' but there wasn't much call for guys like him.

Felix and Marko caught a bus and were on their way to St. Sebastian.

QUEENS

"Mom. the place is real nice. Lotta' trees and grass and you can even see the river from the back side. Benny was working in some flowers when I caught him. He really seems to like it a lot.?

Mom was stirring a sauce and smiling as she listened to MO's description of Saint Sebastian where her oldest son Benny was living.

"He's enough to make you proud, Mom."

"I'm proud of all my boys."

"You only have Benny and me, Mom."

I'm proud of both."

MO sat down. He watched his mother stirring and occasionally sipping and smelling with a wooden spoon the sauce. MO was thinking about her - he loved her – she was getting older – what he was going to talk about with her might hurt her and he didn't want that to happen.

"Mom, I felt real good with Benny."

"You should – he's your little brother."

"Yeah. I know. But he was feeling so good up there and he was making me feel so good I began to think maybe I should go to St..."

The spoon fell in the sauce. Mom turned around, "That's wonderful – that makes me happy – I got to call Mrs...."

"Whoa, Mom, I'm going up there – I'm going to try it out without joining right away. Just hang out with Benny and work with him and see how it goes. He said I could visit any time."

"But you could join..."

"Yeah I could..."

She was fishing the spoon out of the sauce, "That's a good idea."

She kept stirring and MO took a piece of bread and slathered some butter on it and began to munch it. He thought she would be mad but she seemed to like the idea.

"How's the cooking there?"

MO squirmed a little, "Well to tell the truth it isn't much – they don't have a cook."

"What do you eat?"

"Peanut butter, eggs, tuna fish, a lot of crackers and you can go out for Pizza."

She turned and looked at him, she wiped her hands on her apron, "we leave tomorrow – I'm going with you."

* *

MANHATTAN

Dave was back in his chair waiting to face the psychiatrist who had a crush on him. He was hesitant to come back to her, but he owed her money and didn't think it fair to change psychiatrists in mid-stream.

The door opened and Phyllis, the doctor, entered. She was attractive and in another time and world Dave would be interested. Maybe, he thought, after the Saint Sebastian account is settled he might try a date.

She sat across from Dave and smiled, "Good to see you Dave. I was afraid maybe after I...well you know...How I let myself go the last time you were here. I apologize if I...surprised you but I hope you understand that I am attracted to you and I would gladly go out with you any time you request. That is not to say that I cannot serve you and help you come to a more peaceful life by helping you understand some of the things hidden in your psyche that cause you distress. Sitting and talking to you weekly provide comfort for both you and me."

Dave kept nodding as she talked finally he decided he would have to interrupt her, "I'm going to visit St. Sebastians."

"That's a good idea entering into the whole scene of the object of your distress. It will teach you to cope with the problems it's causing you now." She rose from her chair and moved closer to Dave. "I can only wish you the very best and when you return please come see me and we can get a fresh start on your and maybe my life."

"I'm not sure I need a new start."

"Oh, I think you will." She took his hand. He pulled it away and rose from the chair,

"Are you afraid of me, Dave?"

"I am never sure what you will do?"

"I only do what is good for you Dave."

"Well, I think I'll leave." He grabbed his coat and was out the door. He wiped his brow and knew that she was too much for him. He could not go back to her there was no telling what she would do next. He even thought if he should report her but he liked her too much for that.

* *

ST. SEBASTIANS

Albert was away for the week helping the sick priest and Benny was working at the monastery. His favorite thing was working outside with the flowers but, unfortunately, the inside of the monastery need a cleaning too. He had checked the bathrooms they used and they were mopped clean, the halls that he and

Albert walked on were swept and that left him the kitchen. That could become a mess fast.

He opened the door of the kitchen and there was a man! He shouted "What are you doing here?" and he rushed up to him and grabbed him. The man was not big, and he was a lot older than Benny had first thought. "Who are you?"

"Let me go and I will explain."

Benny let him go and the man sat on the table and Benny took a chair. "It better be a good story, because you are not supposed to be here."

The man wore a checkered vest over a loose yellow shirt. He had wool-checkered knickers on and he wore a cap that read 'Jesus Saves.' He had a pleasant face wrinkled with dimples, a small goatee beard, and wire framed glasses on.

"I am Rodney, I know Albert has related my story to you so really it is not necessary for me to retell you the whole story. But the parts that Albert did not stress I am going to mention again. I am condemned, a funny word to use, but all the spirits use it, to remain here until Saint Sebastian arrives at its final destination in history. Its final destination is to be a thriving monastery and I'm not sure that's going to happen for a long time. I have been working and living in this place since my father died two hundred years ago."

Benny was stunned, afraid, he wanted to call 911. He had a first class 'whacko' sitting in front of him talking about having lived at Saint Sebastian for the last two hundred years. He started edging his way to the side of the room where he saw some big knives.

"I know what you're thinking. I'm not going to hurt you. You don't need a knife. I told you I'm a spirit and things like knives and bullets and axes and arrows don't hurt me."

"Albert told me about a ghost..."

"Please don't use the word 'ghost' - spirit is the acceptable word."

63

"Albert told me about you but I really didn't believe him."

"Ohh, you can believe it and just remember that it's not the wind or the mice that makes noise in the night – it's usually me."

"Thanks for telling me."

"I have something else to tell you, Benny, strange things are going to happen here and you have to keep focus but I'll help you."

"What kind of bad things?"

"Oh, I didn't say bad. I said strange. And I think the first one is about to happen right now.

Benny is silent – he looks around the kitchen – "You say right now?"

"Right now."

The bell at the main door started clanging.

"Wow – you scare me."

"Answer the door and we will begin."

Felix and Marko were standing at the front door – they kept looking around to make sure they had not been followed.

"This looks like a very expensive place."

"We are not paying to stay here, Felix, we just join – do the deed and leave."

"Do the deed. I hope Benny is not here at the time, I have known him for a long time – I went to school with his brother   and if I kill him his mother will kill me."

"Felix, we cannot let our personal lives enter this situation. Our necks are on the line and we are going to be dead if we don't come into possession of this joint."

The door opened. Felix and Marko stood there. Benny was dressed in a monk's robe. Marko struggled to speak he finally got his mouth open, "Benny you're all dressed up."

Benny hesitated and stared back. Standing in front of him were two bums, or at least two guys from the old neighborhood whom he never knew to work. He wondered what they were doing here. They certainly wouldn't have come all the way up here for a visit. Would they? Maybe his mother sent them up thinking he would feel better with a visit from some old friends. The one on the left was Felix – he remembered him from the time they had fireworks and he set off a few cherry bombs that almost made him deaf and he had to go to a hospital to get his ears fixed. The other was Marko he lived a few doors away from Benny and he was always a nice guy but a little slow. " Felix, Marko, good to see you. What can I do for you?"

Marko spoke up, "we would like to join."

"Join?"

" That's right Benny. We heard this outfit saves souls and we need our souls and bodies saved."

"Come in." They stepped inside and Benny closed the door behind them, "Follow me."

They sat in one of the parlors near the door. Benny was told that the parlors were used almost every day in the olden times by visitors who frequented Saint Sebastian in the days when they had a large number of men studying.

* *

Felix and Marko were dressed still in their work clothes from the JFK robbery and they looked like they had been slept in for nights, which they had.

"Guys, let me explain," Benny started to speak after they each had taken a seat. "I'm not sure I understand what you mean by saying you would like to join. If you mean join the order of Saint Sebastian then I will tell you we cannot take you just because you walk up to the door and say you want to join. I was here for several weeks before I got to wear this robe and I am not a full

65

postulant yet. I am still in the discerning period and probably will be for some time to come."

"We could start by taking that same period as you", a nervous Marko said.

"We thought about this a long time," four days and night at JFK was a long time to Felix, "and we would really like to give it a try."

Well, Albert, the head of the order, is away and he will be back soon. I suppose I could let you stay here until he returns."

Felix and Marko shrugged.

Benny shrugs and tells them "you can stay the night and we'll see about staying tomorrow.

* *

It is the first night. Felix raps on the door of Marko. Marko comes to the door and Felix tells him he must have the cheap suite on accounta' he's got no bathroom. Marko says, "me neither" they decide to take a look. They tiptoe down the hall - Felix feels a bump

" Take it easy, Marko."

"What's the matter?"

"You keep bumping me."

" I ain't bumping you."

"If you ain't bumpin' me then somebody else is with us."

" We're alone - relax."

Another voice piped up, "What am I? Chopped liver?"

Felix and Marko together: "What's that. Where are you? Somebody is here."

Voice: I'm all around!

Felix and Marko look all around them trying to discover the source of the voice.

The Voice began again. " I want to welcome you to our wonderful way of monastic life."

"We can't see you."

"Of course not. I am a spirit."

"You...you...mean you're a - a- a ghost."

"After Vatican II we dropped "ghost" now we're spirits....except for special occasions."

"Somebody is pulling our leg."

"And they are bumping my shoulder. Let's get outta' here!"

"What about the bathroom?"

"Not necessary anymore!"

Felix waddles down the hall and back to his room followed by a Marko who is slowly turning white with fear.

* *

The next morning Benny got Felix and Marko out of bed – which is exactly what he had to do. They didn't respond to any polite knocks on the door, or loud shouting from the outside. Benny had to go into each room and not only yell "It's way past time to get up" but he had to turn each bed over. Felix and Marko could not believe that it was only 7 o'clock, and Benny informed them that they had to be up by 5:30 every morning,

Felix and Marko were not really awake when they struggled into the kitchen and Benny gave each of them orange juice and cereal from a box.

"Can't I have a little eggs and bacon?," Marko asked.

"This is what you will have every morning – on a special occasion we may have eggs but get to like the cereal."

Felix and Marko ate. Growled. And Benny offered, "you guys can leave, you don't have to stay."

They both looked at each other. In their minds visions of Leo appeared and as if one the answered. "We're staying Benny."

"Good. After you finish eating meet me outside and we can do some   gardening", he started to leave and shouted from the door, "make sure you do the dishes."

* *

By 10:30 Benny had both new novices working pretty good. He smiled to himself several times at the way they worked and he knew he would have to be patient. But most of all he knew that these two bums from the 'hood' were not going to make it.

Benny left them and headed back toward the main house when a BMW pulled up at the front door. Benny stopped and stared at it.

A young guy got out and had three bags and golf clubs with him. He was struggling with them as he headed toward the front door.

Benny called to him, "Can I help you?"

The guy stopped, turned to face Benny and shuffled the bags around until finally he had to set them down. Yes, I want to see Albert."

"Father Albert is not here right now. Can I help you?"

"My name is Dave Fields .I'm a friend of Father Albert's – at least I did some work for him recently, and he's often talked about this place and he has, on several occasions, invited me to come and see it. So here I am."

" We don't have accomodations for visitors – so if you stay – you have to work."

"I don't mind."

"Come with me," Benny led him inside and helped him up the stairs with his baggage. He showed him into one of the regular 'monk' rooms called 'cells.' Dave was a little put-out by the size and décor (which was nothing).

"We have dinner downstairs at 5:30. And I have to apologize for not being more courteous..."

Dave interrupted, "I don't want to be a guest. I want to join for a period of time and live like everyone else here."

Benny stopped, looked him up and down, this guy was not your usual monk – whatever that was – he looked like he had money and position and a BMW, "You want to JOIN the order of Saint Sebastian – become a monk! Did I hear you correctly?"

"You did."

Benny was stunned, "I thought you said you were Albert's friend and wanted to meet him."

"I did say that but I only want to see him to tell him the great change that is coming over my life,"

"Well, get some rest. Meet us downstairs for dinner. Get to bed early we start at 5:30 in the morning."

"Start what."

"Work. And you better tell me your name again."

* *

Benny had an old cow bell which he rang to announce dinner. The bell clanged and banged and made a horrible racket but Felix and Marko dropped what they were doing and headed for the refectory or mess hall as Felix called it.

Felix, Marko, Benny passed by the serving table and placed food on their trays. The meal was stew from a can with large loaves of bread. Benny had prepared it. Felix and Marko and Benny after they took their meals sat at a big table. They were in silence. After a bout 30 full seconds of quiet Marko asked, "Ain't ya' gonna' say a prayer Benny. I want to eat."

"We have another member of the community we have to wait for."

"You mean you got another guy in the joint.?"

'This is a monastery, Felix – not a joint."

Marko was getting edgy – he wanted to eat. "How long do we have to..."

He stopped in the middle of his complaint when Dave walked in. Dave was really dressed for dinner. He wore a purple Armani jacket shiny white pants , Gucci shoes, a soft, off white shirt with a matching purple cravat. He crossed to Benny and the boys and sat down.

Felix and Marko stared at him and Benny spoke up, "You'll notice we don't really get dressed 'up' for dinner. We wear these clothes all the time," and he fingered his monk's robe.

Dave looked scared as he sat with the three others. He watched cautiously as they began to eat their food. Dave looked at the mashed stuff on his plate and thought of the million other places he'd rather be. After a few bites he decided he had to say something, "this is canned stew isn't it?"

"That's right," Benny answered, "we eat as lot of canned stuff here since we have no cook at the present."

Dave nodded his head in agreement, he tried a few more spoonfuls,

"as long as it canned we should really try Dinty Moore's canned stew – it really is better. I once worked on a campaign for them,"

"What do you mean campaign?" Felix asked.

"I worked in an advertising agency and tried to develop reasons why people should eat Dinty Moore's stew rather than another brand."

Everyone was silent and looked at Dave.

Benny chewed his stew slowly,"this stew doesn't taste bad. What do you think brothers."

"Tastes like stew to me," Felix offered.

"Stew is stew," Marko said.

David slipped into his advertising mode and said, "Dinty Moore's is richer with a more beefy taste. It is smoother and offers the freshest vegetables. You really can't compare the quality of Dinty Moore's with this off-brand."

"Your complaints and recommendations are noted and I'll speak to Albert about it."

They finished eating in silence.

Dave decided not to comment on the desert which was store-bought cookies and not 'oreos.'

* *

St. Sebastians main building had 200 rooms. Benny wanted the rooms cleaned. With three guys and himself this was not easy. He assigned Dave to the job and told him to start on the top floor and work his way down. He would have the two helpers. Dave

71

swept the rooms, Marko, mopped them, Felix ran the trash out and kept the mop bucket filled with water.

They were not expected to finish for months since they were interrupted for prayers and classes and the more important cleaning and keeping up of the grounds.

Benny could hardly believe it but they all started working in good spirits and did not complain,

Meals were a problem and Dave never stopped complaining that this catholic food was nothing like the catholic food in the cardinal's residence.

Benny listened patiently to the complaints and promised them all that things would get better. Benny even prayed for food help.

Three days later Goldie and Irish arrived. They had heard that things were slow at St, Sebastians and had no priests. They thought they would give it a shot.

"You either join and are evaluated or you do not – you do not give it a shot. This is not a ping pong team. This is an order of men working to help conditions in the world." Benny almost lost his temper and he would have to get in touch with Albert soon – he didn't think he could take this 'rash' of recruits.

Goldie and Irish dutifully took their places and stepped as awkwardly as the others into Monastic life. It seems that the toughest thing a monk had to do - in the eyes of his recruits – was to get up at 5:30 AM. In some magical, mystical, very strange way they all worked reasonably hard. Benny knew they were not breaking their backs but they were plodding through the daily work and the rooms were getting clean and the grounds were respectful.

* *

Albert returned. Benny met him at the door and ushered him into one of side parlors. He wanted to explain about the new recruits before Albert saw them. He was not quite sure he had done right, but he knew they needed bodies and bodies were coming on the doorstep every day.

Albert sat down and let out as long sigh, "It's not easy being a parish priest, Benny, there are more details and complaints than I thought possible. If I ever heard of a place that lives up to the saying of what's good..." He stopped, stared into the hallway, "Benny I just thought I saw a monk walk by. Benny, did I see a monk walk by?"

"Yes, probably it was Brother Goldie. He had a touch..."

"Brother Goldie? Who the hell is he?

"One of our more recent members."

"I have been gone for two weeks and you mean to tell me you have another man join St. Sebastian's."

"Not exactly. We have five new men."

"Five new men! Where did they come from?"

"I think most of them came from New York City."

"No, I mean why did they suddenly begin appearing. The whole church is crying for people to join and we are on the verge of closing down and we have five recruits! Plus you. Tell me if you think its natural or normal."

Benny shook his head. He had to admit it was strange to him to have so many recruits. Four of them Goldie, Irish, Felix and Marko reminded him of penny ante guys who hung around doing odd jobs for men who controlled certain unions or illegal business' but he couldn't pass judgment on this

Albert spent the next week pondering the strange developments that were developing at Saint Sebastian. Suddenly there were six seminarians - none of them, except Benny, would he have chosen for the life of a priest, seemed legit. He was caught up with the ideas of kicking them out and bringing a sense of sanity to the order or letting them stay on and see where the Holy Spirit led them.

He was letting them stay — at least for a time and turning it over to the Holy Spirit — which was a cop out since he was sure the Holy Spirit had a hell of a lot more important things to deal with.

As long as they were here they would be treated like any other novices follow the regular regimen. Which is why, on a beautiful day in the Spring, he stood before the six and began a lesson in basic, very basic, religion.

Dave, the advertising man, sat in the front of the room, Benny sat next to him. Felix, the handy man, sat towards the rear on the left side, next to Marko, on the right side sat Goldie and Irish.

Albert began, "Lord, we ask you this day to open our hearts and minds to your words that we may come to know you better and serve you with all our hearts."

"Goldie, you did not bless yourself like the other boys.'"

"I ain't a Catholic."

"If you are going to become one of our brothers then you must become a Catholic."

Goldie glanced over at Irish who was mouthing the word ANGEL.

Goldie nodded and spoke," You'se is right — I apologize. I sure want to become a Catholic."

Dave piped up. "As you know, Albert, I am not a Catholic either."

"Yes, I know, Dave, but you did bless yourself."

"I know but I just wanted to let you know I am not a Catholic yet, in case you should say something I'm not supposed to hear."

"Everything I say is open to any religion, any person, any place."

They all nodded.

Albert continued, " You all know we have Ten Commandments and Jesus, when he lived, obeyed these Commandments. But once when Jesus was with his friends one of the friends asked which of these Ten Commandments are the most important."

Felix (Interrupting) "I think it was the honor mother and father one."

"That's very good, Felix. Jesus thought all of them important but he said something different, He said the most important Commandment is to 'Love the Lord your God with all your heart and with all your soul and with all your strength and with all your mind and, 'Love your neighbor as yourself.'"

"These two commandments are at the center of all life and most especially to the life you are stepping into as monks at St. Sebastians."

They all listened in silence. Finally Leo spoke, "love your neighbor as yourself. That may be a little hard when the neighbor leaves all their garbage on your back steps."

"Or makes a racket all night with a radio going full blast."

Albert listened and smiled, "Jesus didn't say you had to like all the things your neighbor did. Just love them in the sense you would have no harm come to them or you would not slander them in any way."

"Slander- is that like cursing them out?"

"Well, just about the same – is means insulting them or telling others they are no good."

Benny asked ,"Who is my neighbor?"

Albert nodded, "That's the same thing that the people talking to Jesus asked. They wanted to know 'Who is my neighbor' so Jesus told them the story of the Good Samaritan. I ll read it to you." Albert picked up a copy of the Bible on the desk and read, "A man was going down from Jerusalem to Jericho, when he fell into the hands of robbers. They stripped him of his clothes, beat him and went away, leaving him half dead. A priest happened to be going down the same road, and when he saw the man, he passed by on the other side. So too, a Levite, when he came to the place and saw him, passed by on the other side. But a Samaritan, as he traveled, came where the man was; and when he saw him, he took pity on him. He went to him and bandaged his wounds, pouring on oil and wine. Then he put the man on his own donkey, took him to an inn and took care of him. The next day he took out two silver coins and gave them to the innkeeper. 'Look after him,' he said, 'and when I return, I will reimburse you for any extra expense you may have.'

"Which of these three do you think was a neighbor to the man who fell into the hands of robbers?"

 The expert in the law, who had asked Jesus, replied, "The one who had mercy on him." Jesus told him, "Go and do likewise."

They all nodded at the story and Albert continued, "so that means everybody is really your neighbor.

Benny put up his hand and Albert recognized him, "I think it is better to say 'love the world as yourself.'

"Good idea, Benny, if only we could learn to do this."

* *

QUEENS

MO had worked all day on a sink over on 89th street. Fixing a sink is not usually that hard but the tenant's sink had backed up and caused a flood in the floor below and then the floor below that...three floors got involved. These old buildings could use the plumbing redone completely. He meant all over,

The buildings were built at least 75 years ago and nobody had paid much attention to the water pipes in all that time. He would find patches (supposed to last for 48 hours) still on pipes and he remembered one repair he found with the patch box lying beside it and a date on the box of 1938. There were probably thousands and thousands of pipes all over Queens with the same tell tale boxes lying around. He knew he couldn't fix them all – just one at a time – and his work was probably guaranteed forever.

He thought 'how great' it was to live at home – the same home he grew up in. His mother did all the cooking for him and cleaned the house – he did his own laundry and gave his mother a few bucks a week for board. But he was 28 and knew he had to get his own place soon.

He thought of Benny a lot lately – he did it – he got a place. He broke away and seemed to be enjoying it. Benny spoke to him about a different level of thinking he was getting involved in, Benny had turned from a low level drifter in the accounting business to a kind of guy, that according to him, "had found himself."

MO wasn't sure what finding yourself meant. He thought about it and decided to stop for a beer before getting home, He stopped in at Greg Luzzi's place and ordered a Red Line. He liked this beer and it felt lighter and cleaner than the heavy German Beers, Bumper was the bartender. She had been a few years ahead of MO in High School. Ole Bumper had married and then divorced and now bartended – her real name was Lucy Riviera.

She greeted him with a great smile, "How you doin', handsome?"

She dug down and came with a Red Line.

"I'm still makin' it," he held up the Red Line and shook his head in a kind of disbelief, "four bucks for this little bottle."

'Yeah, but you got company, me, and its good beer," and Bumper gave him a big wink and smile. "Been out to Shea lately, 4 bucks for a beer is like manna from heaven compared to their prices."

"That's different."

"Look, MO, you can talk to me. You can't talk to the team out there."

"It's a lot - I still remember the 50 cent glass."

"I didn't think you were that old."

"Hell, Bumper, you can remember that too."

"You know, MO, I spend a lot of time in my life not remembering things, like Harold the Husband, Dominic the divorce lawyer,and Greg the illustrious owner of this dump."

"I thought you had a kid, too"

Bumper was silent and she moved to the other end of the bar. MO guessed he had hit a soft spot in Bumper. He nursed his drink for a while hoping she would see her way to come back down his end of the bar. People got hurt and MO knew it - he hated when he slipped and backed up people. Bumper was coming towards him. She stopped and faced him head-on.

"MO, you've known me since High School - you know I've got a kid a nine years old and he's a doll – and I know he needs a father but he's got a mother and he's doing good."

"Bumper, I didn't mean anything."

"Yeah, but it's not the thing I like to hear. People, well I guess my parents and brothers and sisters are the worst about saying things, They keep yelling at me for working here and, according to them, ruining my life. What the hell do they know about me? Sure I could do better. How about you, MO, could you do better? You want to do better and live better. Don't you?"

"Sure..."

"If you had a kid people would be asking you all the time about him or her. But you don't have a kid so you're safe. Want another Red Line?"

"Yeah, sure." She gave him the Red Line and answered Augie Goetz at the other end of the bar with a loud 'keep you shirt on Augie – Puleez keep your shirt – there are ladies present."

MO sipped his Red Line. Did Benny have to put up with this kind of life. Probably if Benny became a priest he would be able to console people like Bumper. I guess bein' a priest makes people sit and take notice more. Then he started thinking. Can you learn to be a priest? MO didn't think so. He figgered people were born with it like Derek Jeter and that painter Picasso. They were just able to play shortstop and paint - some kind of gift from God. And when he listened to people like Bumper he wanted to help but he didn't know where to start. There was nothing wrong with her and people, like him, didn't have any right to criticize them.

He left ten bucks on the bar and left.

He walked to 226th and turned left to his house. He noticed a sign on the front porch. He was still about five houses away and he couldn't read it. When he got close enough it read "ROOMS FOR RENT."

What the hell is going on. Did mom decide to rent Benny's room or maybe his. What the hell was for rent.

He opened the door walked in smelled the dinner. It ws going to be great but what the hell, "Mom what's with the sign on the front 'For Rent.'"

"MO, I'm glad you're home, We have a delicious dinner for you."

"The sign mom. The sign. What's with the sign."

"I'm renting all the rooms – except yours of course – you can keep yours."

"That's nice Ma. But where are you going?"

"With Benny."

"Ma, Benny is working at being a priest. He has to live with a bunch of men they don't allow women to live there."

"I can arrange it."

"Somehow I believe you might be able to – but what the heck are you going to do there."

"I'm going to cook."

"Cook!"

"Benny told me they don't have a cook and you went there and told me you had to eat out most of the time and Benny was trying to cook. Well, I am going to be their new cook."

"What about me?'

"You could come and visit and on those days we'll have something very special from among your favorites."

"Come and visit."

They sat down to eat. MO had the wind knocked out of him. His mother was joining up. He asked his mother for another bowl of pasta fasulla. His mind went back to Bumper and his thoughts while sipping the Red Line.. What the heck I got some of those feelings about helping others, too. "I'm coming with you, Ma."

* *

SAINT SEBASTIAN'S

Back at St. Sebastians Goldie and Irish were taking a break from their "latrine duty" and had climbed to the top of the building. There was a walkway around the edge of the roof and a building in the center. They didn't realize it but the building was a miniature observatory built years ago when the seminarians took courses in astrology and spent time reviewing the skies and the endlessness of God's creation.

Around the walk was an iron fence to protect anyone from falling. Goldie and Irish were leaning on the fence discussing business.

Irish shook his head slowly and spoke, This is getting to be a bigger job than just knocking off a priest, I count about ten guys here - counting us."

Goldie starts counting on his fingers – he comes up with ten. Then he smiles) "Yeah, there's ten here but we ain't gonna' knock ourselves off!"

"That's true but that is still more than I figgered."

"Look it ain't a ridiculous number we just got to make it look like an accident - and 'swoosh' all of them are gone."

"What's with swoosh?"

The Voice speaks, " He means all at once."

Goldie nodded, "Exactly."

Irish nodded, "my favorite is the subway push but that is out. No subways."

"How about a window shove."

The voice spoke again, " Eight guys at once. Never work."

"I agree."

"You agree with what, Irish?"

"Like you said - eight guys at once would never work."

" I never said that."

"Yes you did."

" I did not."

The voice interrupted, " Don't argue. I did."

"What the hell is that, Irish?

"Somebody's here Goldie? Who are you?

" A friendly spirit!"

Both Irish and Goldie pull back from the fence and stare at each other for thirty seconds or more then finally Goldie speaks." I think there is a strange thing happening here, Irish."

"It is not a good idea for us to continue our discussion, Goldie."

They both head for the roof exit and fight their way back to the bathrooms to continue mopping.

* *

Benny was working in the chapel as far as he knew all the other fellows were working in the fields or on the grounds. Albert was in his office looking at bills. Benny was a little surprised that Albert has just taken all the new recruits in his stride – he didn't seem worried about any of them. Benny was sure it was too strange – all those guys storming the gates and wanting to join after a couple of years of no new novices – Benny said no way.

The front door bell rang. Benny was the person who had to answer since the chapel was just across from the main entrance. Everytime Benny had answered the door, it seemed to him, another recruit for St. Sebastians was there asking to join. He girded himself and swung open the door.

"Mom!"

"So, invite me in. I've come to be your new cook."

"Our new cook? We didn't hire a cook."

"Hired. I'm not for hire. I am just giving my life to God and the kitchen. I am going to cook."

"Giving?"

"That's right, 'Giving' free for the rest of my life. MO is getting stuff out of the car – he's going to join.

"Hi Benny," MO shouted from down in the driveway, "I've come to stay."

"What the hell is going on?"

Mom looked at Benny, " Such language from a boy who is going to become a first class priest."

"MO, you want to join."

MO struggled up the stairs with some boxes of pots and pans, "When Ma said she was joining up I had no cook – so here I am."

"That is not the reason to join the order."

"Aww, I know Benny, but it's been bothering me for a long time - ever since I visited you months ago and realized it's not such a bad life and I don't want to fix pipes in Queens no more – so here I am."

* *

That night Benny lie awake in his 'cell' thinking of the day's events.

The new cook – he felt real good and it was certainly the best meal he had since coming to St. Sebastian's – delicious home made egg plant parmigana. Ten minutes after his mother arrived she had made the whole thing from scratch and served it at 6 PM. She was certainly an asset, but why was she here? His father had died four years ago and she was lonely but he never suspected she was this lonely! He thought she was obviously doing it to be near himself but along came MO and God Knows that if MO ever liked this place – St Sebastian's would be stuck with entire family. He put aside the idea that she might leave after she discovers there's no bingo or card parties here and the Senior Citizens did not meet on the grounds.

MO was just a quick knee-jerk reaction. He was certain of this, But if he was wrong and he did stay – what was Albert going to think?

Benny tossed in bed and was sure it would work itself out. But in the meantime he was uncomfortable with all the other recruits - much more uncomfortable with them than he was with his family. They were a real mystery to him – guys like that just didn't run out and commit to a celibate life with no money – they for sure did not!

* *

The next morning the entire personnel of St. Sebastian's sat down to a breakfast of pancakes (with or without blueberries), bacon, and coffee that actually tasted like coffee. The new cook got nothing but praised showered on her from every corner. And she smiled at the wonderful reception and thought to herself, " I finally found real appreciators for my cooking - I should have come here years ago."

Leo, Irish, Benny, MO, Felix, and Goldie all had seconds. David passed on seconds – he was still working on his weight.

After breakfast the boys brought the dishes to the kitchen and Ma Kicked them out – she would not let them wash dishes. They all thought she was being nice – and she was – but she had also met Rodney that morning. He was the first ghost Ma ever met and he was very polite and well mannered. She wanted to talk to him more in private and he had agreed to help with the clean up. Ma set him to work and began with the questions. She wanted to know if he had ever met her darling husband up there in the blue skies of heaven and was very disappointed when he told her he hadn't.

Rodney explained that he was an angel – he had been an angel since before time began and never worked in the human world before so he had little chance of running into people from earth. "But," he told her, " that doesn't mean he's not there. So I wouldn't worry about him."

Ma shook her head as she scraped plates, "I'd hate to think of him as going to the other place."

Rodney was putting away the butter and syrup and said, "You are not to worry about him – just remember him and pray for him – the rest is taken care of. I don't think he's in the other place."

"Well, I hope he's not. But he was a cursing, drinking man and had little regard for Sunday services."

Rodney nodded, "happens to a lot of people, but they manage to get through – I'm putting the coffee in the freezer I read it keeps fresher."

Goldie and Irish were working together in the laundry downstairs. All the residents got clean sheets and pillow cases once a week and the two of them were assigned the task by Benny. Irish got to thinking that he had an Aunt Mushy (that wasn't her real name, but everybody called her that on account of a pie she made called 'mushy') and she worked in a laundry for 8.75 an hour which was more than he was making working in this laundry. He was shoving sheets into a washing machine and he looked over at Goldie and thought "this is not right - this is not the reason we came here."

He caught Goldie's attention, " We have got to start causing some calamities around here because I am not in my right "conscious" to take any more of those Sunday school classes."

Goldie shook his head and answered "Agreed - even tho' I have never heard of such a thing as my spiritual life what does he mean like when I dream or somethin'..."

"Forget about it... C'mon, finish here and come with me."

They finished filling the machines and turned them on and then sneaked out the door.

"Why we sneaking, Goldie?"

"I don't want anybody to see us."

"Oh...but why?"

"It will take the mystery out of it."

Irish led Goldie to a door with a narrow set of stairs going almost straight up.

"Where are we, Irish?"

"On our way to fulfill our destiny."

They climbed in silence and came out on the roof of the main building.

"What is our destiny""

"To be here with these." Irish reached into the corner and hidden under a canvas were two old rifles.

"If you can remember, Goldie, we were sent her to acquire this place following the death of all known individuals who may dispute a claim on these vacant – except for us – properties."

"But before proceeding, Goldie. I have a problem."

"Problem? What's bothering you, Irish. Nothing serious 'cause I got to put my best concentration on the subject in question."

"Have you signed anything?"

"Whaddya' mean?"

" Who knows we are here."

Goldie(putting up gun), "Angel - he sent us."

"Knocking all these holy rollers off ain't gonna' do us any good unless we also inherit the place."

"Doya' mean we gotta' wait."

"Till we get enlisted or whatever they do."

" Dammit, Irish..."

Irish interrupts, "Watch your language, Goldie."

"You mean Dammit is wrong."

"You are suggesting that a person or thing be sent to hell."

"Aw C'mon – that doesn't..."

Irish stops him, "you will blow our cover."

Goldie is silent he turns and replaces the rifles under the old canvas.

"Now don't you feel better, Goldie."

"It's not my feelings it's Angel's feelings that have me concerned."

* *

Later that morning a car pulled into the driveway and parked in the garage. Albert was back. He immediately got together with Benny.

"Your mother is the cook!"

"Well, she arrived yesterday and insisted on cooking for us young men. She is taking no money – it is all volunteer."

"What about your brother?"

"He is a new student. He claims he was thinking about joining for some time and when Mom decided to come here that was a sign."

Albert sat down. "Benny, what is going on here. I go away and you open the door to another prospect and a cook! I look at all the men who have indicated in some way that they want to be seminarians. Benny, they do not look like seminarians."

"What does a seminarian look like, Albert?"

Albert nodded. "I don't know." He looked away and noticed Felix and Marko raking in the garden. "I guess they look like...well, like anybody."

"Do you want me to tell them that have to leave. I can just say we've had problems and they better all go home."

Albert was silent. After a few minutes he spoke, "We'll let them stay here a while longer then later we'll reevaluate."

* *

The next morning Albert met all the "guests" in one of the class rooms on the first floor. He rose and spoke, "St. Sebastians welcomes all of you. It has been so hard in the past few years and now to welcome this wonderful group of candidates is such a joy - you bring much peace to my heart. We have so much work to do, with you at my side I am sure we can achieve our mission. I know all of you have been working hard at the many chores for the last few days but we must continue studies in trying better to understand the mysteries of our religion."

Benny sat in the classroom along with the others. Benny had studied many things in his months with Albert and he was all ready to learn more. He really was sincerely on the path to become a priest. The others looked like kids in a Sunday School class. They were slouched in their chairs and bored to the gills before class even started.

Mo was the only student who seemed to have the slightest interest. He and David did not have a hidden mission – the others were mulling in their minds various ways to do what they were 'sent' to do.

Goldie was doodling – drawing little pictures of guns with big "bang" balloons coming out of the barrels.

Albert began,"Today we'll talk about 'Forgiveness' – So many times each one of us has probably done something to a friend or enemy or even a member of our own family that has hurt them. Usually we are sorry for that thing we may have done and we ask to be forgiven. That is all good but what happens to us when the person we have hurt does not want to forgive us. We get angry – we might even want to 'get even' and hurt them back. What do you fellows think of that?"

He was met with silence. Then he said. "What do you think?" and he pointed at Felix.

Felix was quiet, he screwed up his lip and was trying to talk but his face resembled a screw driver, then after a few beats he spoke, "If a guy turns on me I just get even with him and forget about it."

"How do you get even with him?"

"I'm not too sure ya' want to hear that."

Albert smiled. "We're all friends here. You can tell us."

"I ain't too sure."

"I know Felix a long time," Marko spoke up, "he wouldn't hurt a flea...so I bet he gives the guy a handshake and says he won't hurt him again."

Irish laughed.

"What's funny, Irish? Albert asked.

"I think he is wrong about Felix."

"What do you mean?"

"I think, Felix, would stomp on the guy and not shake his hand."

Marko quietly spoke, "Do not give him any ideas, Irish?"

Irish stood up. Felix stood up. Marko stood up, Goldie stood up.

Benny stood up and said, "sit down gentlemen right now."

Felix turned to Marko, his fists clenched.

"Sit down, Now.

Everybody sat down.

Benny turned to Albert, "Sorry for the interruption, Father."

"Well, yes, er well I was going to read a passage from Matthew."

"Okay, let's hear what Matthew has to say about forgiveness," Goldie asked.

Albert began, "Peter, you remember him, he was the leader of the apostles?"

Goldie spoke, "Apostles?"

"They were the guys who hung out with Jesus," Irish said.

"Peter asked Jesus, 'How many times should I forgive someone who does something wrong to me? Is seven times enough?"

"Seven times – he has to be kidding," Marko piped up.

Benny stood up and declared "Marko, no interruptions until Albert finishes reading all of the story." He slowly looked at all the 'students' and declared quietly and firmly, "Now all of you, just relax and let's hear the rest."

"So back to Matthew," Albert spoke, " Jesus answered Peter, not just seven times but seventy seven times."

"Is he kidding?" said Irish, "my old lady would..."

"Enough, Irish, we have to hear the story," Benny ordered.

Albert went on, " One day a king decided to call in all the officials who worked for him and asked them to give him an accounting of all they owed the king. One official owed the king fifty million silver coins. The king ordered him to be sold as a slave along with his wife and children and everything he owned in order to pay the debt.

"The official fell on his knees and began begging, 'have pity on me and I will pay you back every cent I owe," the king felt sorry for him and let him go free. The king even told his men that he did not have to pay back the money.

Goldie, Irish, Marko, Felix, and David gave a round of applause to this generosity.

"But that's not the end," Benny interrupted the clapping, "there's more – go on, Father."

"Thanks, Benny, the most important part of the story is next,"

Albert said, " The man got up and left – no more debt. As he was walking he ran into another man who owed him money. He grabbed the man and started choking him, 'pay me the money you owe me or else' but the poor man had no money. He called the officials and had the man thrown in jail until he was able to pay what he owed."

People found out about this and told the king what had happened. The king was really mad and he called the man whose debt he had forgiven back. He said to him, 'You are an evil man – when you begged for mercy I said you did not have to pay back a cent – don't you really think you should have shown pity to someone else. The king was so angry he ordered the official to be tortured until he could pay back everything he owed."

Then Jesus said to the officials gathered, " that is how my father in heaven will treat you, if you don't forgive each of my followers with all your heart."

The class was silent.

Albert asked, " what do you think?' He looked around the faces of the men who all had a look of disbelief on their faces. "Goldie, what do you say?"

Goldie said, "I dunno, I just think the guy was a nut to push his luck."

Felix piped up, " I guess the guy got what was comin' to him."

"Do you men forgive others for what they do to you."

Marko spoke, "I ain't gonna lie. If a jerk does me wrong - I'm gonna' get even. 'Even Steven' is the name of my game. I figger that's fair."

Albert shook his head, "but don't you think, Marko, that if you forgive someone for what he does then that person you forgave should forgive others."

"Albert, most of my life I think I been unfair and I don't forgive people – I take care of them in a special way," Marko who had stood up when he first talked – sat down.

Irish was shaking his head, "I'm not sure of that whole thing. I can give a guy a break if he gives me a break but I never heard of forgiving somebody 77 times. Maybe once or twice – maybe even 8 or 9 times but not 77."

Albert sighed, "No, he doesn't really mean 77 times. He is speaking in a metaphor which...."

The word metaphor set off a chain reaction of 'looks'.

Benny jumped to his feet, "I think we've had enough today, Albert, We'll continue tomorrow after lunch." He quickly shooed the boys out of the room – he definitely did not want Albert to tangle himself up explaining a metaphor.

They all left.

* *

Goldie and Irish were outside walking toward the river. They wanted to be alone to discuss their duties, which was beginning to bother them both.

Goldie, a little worried and sounding mad said, " I ain't goin' to no school. I got kicked out in the seventh grade once - I don't want to do it over again. It was hard on my mother - I get kicked out again she might die."

"You got a mother?"

"What you think I was - one of those virgin births?"

"You once was a little boy?"

Goldie stopped walking and stared at Irish, "What's so strange about that - what the hell were you a little elephant?"

Irish replied a little louder, "Hey - don't insult my youth."

"...Or the elephants."

At that outburst Irish grabbed Goldie by the collar and was about To rough him up but Albert came around the corner of building and saw the action, "Problem?.

Goldie calming down quickly, " We was just gettin' excited about school."

Irish in a quiet voice, "Albert, do we need a loose leaf book or what ...?'

Albert smiled and left them.

* *

QUEENS

Fiddler worked for Big Leo in his stationery, novelty, newspaper, chewing gum, etc. store. He handled the every day customers who were in and out buying all day long. In the back of the store Leo had his office for a whole different business – a business that definitely did not require a front door facing the street.

Fiddler sorted through the mail. Usually he was able to take care of everything that came in. He sent the bills to the accountant, he ordered whatever he needed for the store, however, the mail today featured a letter from the police department. Big Leo did not like this kind of mail – the mere mention of police would sometimes set him off on a cursing campaign that was scary. Fiddler thought about it and then decided to open it. He took one look at the note and decided to interrupt Leo and show it to him.

He knocked on Leo's door and waited. He knocked again- still no response from inside. Fiddler knew he might risk a screaming attack but he knocked again.

"Get the hell in here – you moron – you know I do not like to be disturbed with matters of the candy store," the booming and blasting voice of Big Leo came through the door.

Fiddler slowly opened the door.

"Well, what is it, Fiddler – out with it and it better be good."

93

Fiddler crossed over and handed Big Leo the note from the police department, "I thought you'd like to see this."

Leo grabbed the note and is jaw dropped, "Those no good rotten stupid jerks – they actually left my truck at the airport."

Fiddler nodded, "about six months ago."

"The police want $12,678 in fines and fees."

"What should I do, Mr. Leo?"

"First, call 'Petey Z', give him the plate number of the truck and a description of the truck , and tell him I want it stolen from the police right away. Soon as he has the truck tell the 'the book' to cut a check and go get the truck – when the police can't find it we won't have to pay." Second - find out where those two monks who are supposedly arranging a big deal for me are then get my car and driver - we are going to visit those two monks in the woods."

Fiddler left. Big Leo sat behind his desk. He was thinking of how so many jerks worked for him – he was going to clean house and start getting rid of dead wood,

Fiddler cam back in, "Mr. Leo, Petey Z, thinks this job is going to be tough and he's not sure...

"Is he on the phone?"

"Yeah"

Leo picked up the phone, "Petey Z, what the hell kind of thief are you? Get me my truck. Now. I do not want to hear about problems

I got enough of them. – Just get me the truck. Now."

Petey Z's voice came over the phone, "But they probably got it under lock and key and guarded."

"Soo you telling me you never stole something under lock and key and guarded??

"No, but this is the police..."

"And this is Leo. Get the truck." And he slammed the phone down.

* *

ST. SEBASTIANS

Albert usually sat alone afternoons quietly saying prayers. Actually he was praying for help in what to do with his new 'novices.' He kept asking himself, "Who were they? Why were they here?" They were certainly not the average type of seminarian he remembered from his days of study. Of course nothing was the same as then. The whole world was so darn mixed up that he kept thinking that maybe the new church, the church of the twenty-first century, would have to depend on the type of men that had come to Sebastians. They were ignorant of basic truths but they seemed in some odd way interested in staying.

He had been looking out towards the river and watching a train pass on the other side heading south and a boat heading north and several late small sail boats crossing back and forth. When he was interrupted.

"Albert, can I talk to you."

He turned it was David. David was a bit apart from the other recruits but still he didn't seem exactly right. "Certainly, David, sit down."

David sat next to him.

"This is a lot different from the last time we met, Albert...er ,or should I say, Father Albert."

"Albert is fine. I must say, David, I was certainly surprised when I discovered that you had joined us. I had no idea you were thinking of such a thing.

"Well, really it was my psychiatrist who suggested I visit."

"Your psychiatrist! That is not a good reason to come to St. Sebastian's. I really think you have to reconsider..."

"But I like it here."

"That's very nice, David, but we do not run a hotel. Usually we train men to become priests. Although it seems since I have returned and looked at all the recruits Benny let in the door – I am not sure what we are running."

"That's just it. I know it's not a hotel – I know what is here – and I am surprised by the fact that I am pretty sure I want to be a priest or a religious brother."

"What will your psychiatrist say to such an idea?"

"I don't think she'll like it at all."

"Exactly. She's going to label it a very rash act. Becoming a member of our community is a life commitment and really requires a long and thorough discerning process."

"You make it seem a lot more than 'just joining.' I'm not sure she knew about that. She's going to be pissed about a long process."

"I'm sure she's a good lady down deep, David, she'll understand and you can help her."

"I'm not so sure. She jumped out of the chair after me one day. I swear she was trying to rape me."

Rape you! My God, that's hard to believe. What was she thinking?"

"I think she was thinking what all rapists are thinking."

"Was she upset or angry?"

"She was very very very upset because her father

took her out of the party scene when she was a kid – all because she got a 94 and not a 100 in junior year Math – she was never allowed any boy friends – ever."

Albert shook his head in disbelief, "and she became a psychiatrist ?"

"That's right."

"I think, you're well to be away from her."

"But now its different. I think I really want to stay...stay here I mean – not got back to her."

Albert took some time, he had to think about David. He liked him but this young man was confused. Albert knew he was accustomed to large cars and expensive restaurants and probably beautiful women. He had a long way to go if he were ever to become a serious candidate for the religious life. He decided to let him to stay for a few months and maybe he will be able to make some kind of discernment.

" David, give me more time to think more about your request to stay."

"Good. And thanks, Albert, You'll be pleased."

"I hope so."

"Thanks, Albert. We'll talk again."

He got up to leave and Albert bid him goodbye. When he was a few feet away Albert said, " She really tried to rape you?"

David turned back, " She sure did." And he left.

Albert sat shaking his head in disbelief

* *

The next morning Benny was out on the main road leading to the monastery picking up mail. A big Cadillac, shiny and pristine. about twenty years old, was parked just beyond the gate - Somebody had spent a fortune in making it look brand new. The man driving leaned out the window and called him, "Hi, Father could you help me?"

Benny was dressed in a monk's robe but he was not yet a priest, "I'm not a 'father' but maybe I can help."

"Is this the St. Sebastian place.?"

"Yes, it is can I help you?"

"We are looking for two guys, who owe my friend, Big Leo, a truck.

We would like to speak to Marko and Felix."

"They are busy right now." Benny was not sure where Marko and Felix were but these two men seemed a little strange to Benny – a little like 'enforcers or collectors.' Guys in the old neighborhood who happened to welsh on a bet or owed one of the big guys money would send a couple of people like this to collect.

"We are here at the behest of Big Leo who is not happy about losing his truck."

The man sitting next to the driver who hadn't spoke yet in a low growly voice said, "We will be honest wid ya' – Big Leo has located the truck but nevertheless it cost him a big piece of change due to de fact that the clown Marko and the fruitcake Felix have not in the past been very diligent."

"Aahh", thought Benny this is the reason Felix and Marko are here – they have obviously caused a problem for 'Big Leo' and they are hiding out. St Sebasitan is their refuge in a storm. He immediately thought to expose them, but if he did they both might be severely hurt at the least. He felt sure Albert would protect them and so would he, "Well, gentlemen, the best I can tell you is that Brother Felix and Brother Marko are not available."

The driver interrupted, "They ain't brothers or at least I know they got different 'old men' - Marko's daddy got hit by an ice truck years ago and Felix lived next to me when he was in school."

The other man said, "Can't we just go in the gates and talk to them for as few minutes."

The driver added, "We'll just take a few minutes."

Benny turned and closed the entrance gate and locked it. "Sorry not today."

The Driver shouted, "Big Leo is gonna' be mad."

Benny did not turn back and he could hear the car leave.

* *

Benny was confused. It was becoming obvious to him that Brother Felix and Brother Marko were running away from something. Running away? He thought about himself. Wasn't he running away from something? Was that a reason to become a religious brother?

He decided to take a walk, there was a path, Albert had once told him about the path, and it wove in and out about the forest section of the Monastery's grounds. The founders had created it for meditation. Albert explained that he often took it when he wanted to really think something out. It was good to be alone.

Felix and Marko were obviously hiding from something - that was not a good reason to join.

But what about his own reasons? Stuck in the middle of Queens with no place to go just plain bored. He ran away – didn't he? There wasn't an awful lot of religion in him when he started. All his religion came from the fat nun Alberta and the skinny priest Finnegan. But he came here – he just saw the ad. The ad made him think and now he was more and more certain everyday that this was really where he belonged.

He wasn't sure of his brother and he wasn't sure of his Mom or wherever she fit in? Nor the new guy David.

But he was certain about Felix, Marko, Goldie, and Irish They were definitely different.. Different? But shouldn't they have a chance to change their ways - Albert had told him many times that "You never know who may be called from the accountant to the zoo keeper. We are all entitled to a chance to change our lives. And hadn't Albert struggled explaining to the boys how many times you could be forgiven and if they had done something very wrong then they all knew they could be forgiven,

Then the other side of Benny started that maybe these guys would attract men who use things like guns and clubs to enforce their ideas. Wouldn't the whole monastery be put in danger? Was he under an obligation to tell Albert what he felt? Maybe? But he knew one thing he was not going to do it right away – they all deserved a chance to come around and follow the rules and become members of the order like himself.

He went over to the kitchen to see his Mom - it was almost time for dinner.

* *

David had tried to pray after his meeting with Albert but every time he got going he thought of nothing but the psychiatrist and 'Baby" and what they were doing now and shouldn't he be with them having a good time. He never thought of the agency and he could pray around that all day but praying around the girls that was still tough.

Gold and Irish were finishing up a game of mumbly-peg. The game where you kept throwing a knife held different ways and make it stick in the ground. Goldie was into Irish for $157.50 – they bet on every toss in every game.

Goldie was it sure it was happeningl because of the knife, "The next time we use my knife."

"The knife makes no difference, Goldie – it is the finesse – I think you call it."

"Well I got to get me some of the Fin...whatever."

"You only get it from practice, Goldie."

Goldie missed the jack in the box (one of the ways you have to toss the knife into the ground) "Dam it. Give me another try.

A bell rang and Irish picked up the knife, " It's time for dinner."

Mom served pork chops and homemade applesauce

And everybody said grace and then licked their platters clean.

* *

LEO'S OFFICE

"I'm telling you Leo – we could not get in. You remember Benny the kid who use to live out a ways was there with a priest robe on and he wouldn't let us in."

Leo looked at him and took three puffs from an unlighted cigar and asked, "I suppose you knocked gently and inquired the presence of the boys."

"That is right."

Leo held up the the parking fines, "You realize of course that this more than 12 grand that those two ass holes have got me on the hook for."

Fiddler cowered a little and quietly spoke, "I know."

"You know."

"I know."

"This is not acceptable. You hear me. You should have busted the gates open and dragged those two clowns out just so I could kill them."

"But Leo it looks like a holy place."

101

"You want to know another 'holy place' – I'll tell you one. It is the cemetery on Green Lawn Avenue – that is a holy place – and that where all you guys are going to be resting if I don't get those two clowns, assholes, jerks, meatballs, and whatever – I cannot think with this damn cigar not lit....

Fiddler leaned forward with a lighter, "You want to light it?"

"My old lady would kill me if she finds out I smoked - it is driving me crazy and I don't need shmoes like Felix and Marko causing me to get upset and losing my temper."

"I won't tell her you smoked."

"What the hell is wrong with you, Fiddler, ain't you got no honor. I told her I won't smoke and I won't."

The phone rang and Big Leo picked it up.

"Yeah....yeah........yeah..............yeah......They what ....yeah.... yeah yeah....yeah....I'll talk." He slammed the phone down.

"Fiddler, that was my lawyer, Do you know I pay him $100 for every ten minutes he talks to me – that is $600 an hour and he tells me he is cheap."

"Wow – that is a lot."

"I can go to jail for taking a one dollar from a humble man on the street to cover a number that will pay him $200 and that effin' lawyer sticks me for $300 every ten minutes and he is an 'effin pillar of society."

"I'm sorry Big Leo."

"He has just informed me that the damn truck ain't worth $12 grand and the police still want the money and they think the truck was stolen, which it was, but they still want the money and they are going to get it. And furthermore why it was it parked in a restricted area of Kennedy airport and the lawyer thinks I may be a terrorist.

I can't take it anymore I am going to bust down the gates of that holy place and drag those two 'effin cupcakes "outa there. Get the car!

* *

ST. SEBASTIAN

Father Timmons was the pastor of a church not too far from St. Sebastians. Over the years he and Albert had become close friends.. They got together once a week and Albert always took masses for him when he was called away.

Father Timmons was 92 and had no living relatives. He lived alone and members of his church provided him with two meals a day – he still made his own breakfast. Many times Albert would invite 'Timmons' over to the monastery for evening meals. Timmons had never tasted the cooking of Ma and tonight was his night.

With a bit of fear and lots of trepidation Albert brought Father Timmons into the dining room. All the boys, as Albert referred to them, were there.

Albert stood up and spoke "Brothers, tonight we have as our guest Father Timmons from nearby St. Raymond's church as our guest. Father prefers to be called 'Timmons' – I would too if my first name was Aloysius."

All the guys nodded agreement except Irish who declared "I always thought ' Allwishes' was a girl's name."

Timmons replied, "Oh no indeed not, Aloysius was a wonderful saint. He died when he was very young – he led a very holy life."

Albert smiled, "Oh, yes, brother Irish, and all of us could do well if we remembered he once said, 'I am but a crooked piece of iron and have come into religion to be made straight by the hammer of forgiveness.' Now, Lord, we thank you for our food and life, and may all those without food have something to eat tonight."

They all began to eat and many of them thought of the crooked piece of iron.

* *

After dinner Timmons went to the kitchen to thank Ma. Rodney was there. Timmons had met Rodney several times and like everyone else did not understand him. He really did seem to Timmons like a person who could do strange things but he was not the picture of an angel and never would be.

"That was a fine and delicious meal, Ma," beamed Timmons.

Ma thanked him profusely and promised him that she would visit his church someday. They chatted for a bit about Italy and Ireland and the grandeur of the 'old' countries and the recklessness of the people today who seemed to care little for how they treated people and things.

Albert entered," C'mon Timmons I have to drive you home – unless you want to spend the night."

Timmons did not want to spend the night. He thanked everybody again and left.

After he had gone Rodney looked at Ma sadly, "If you want to go hear him say mass – I would go soon."

"Why, Rodney?"

"It's just a good idea, Ma."

* *

The next afternoon Felix and Marko had all the garden raked and were cursing at leaves as they fell on their work

FeliX leaned on his rake and spoke quietly, "what do you think 'all wishes' meant by saying he was a crooked piece of iron and was being made straight by a hammer."

"Not a hammer. The hammer of forgiveness."

"What you think it means?"

"I think it means 'forgiveness' can make just about anything that's in bad shape better."

"Not a real hammer?"

Marko nodded, "its just as way of saying that forgiveness is very very strong."

Felix nodded and frowned, "I think I get it. Let's go it's time to eat.

They put away their rakes and left.

* *

After dinner that night they started talking about Father Timmons and saints.

"Okay Benny, What is it with these saints?" It was Felix asking.

"What are they? What do they do?"

Goldie shook is head and said, "I never thought they were real – I just thought they were the names of people."

Benny smiled and answered, "They are the names of people. They once lived on earth and now are dead."

"I know everybody is not a saint – because my old man kept telling me I was not and never will be a saint," Irish added.

"In my old religion we did not have many saints – I never heard much about them at all."

"In most Christian religions there are saints, but not like the ones in the Catholic religion – we have thousands of saints - actually

more likely millions of saints.," Benny answered.

"Millions?"

"Well," Benny said, "Everybody who has died is potentially a saint. But some men and women who have led very good lives and done many good things for society we call them saints and we ask them in our prayers to ask God to help us. So after you die, Felix, if many people around you think that you led a very very good life friends and people you know will tell others. Finally it gets into the mind of priests and Cardinals and Popes and they begin asking God to help them understand Felix's life better and then one day they tell everybody and you are St. Felix."

"How about that, " Marko said, " I could hardly believe it Felix a saint. My old lady wouldn'ta minded me hanging out with you at all."

David interjected. "He isn't a saint yet."

Benny smiled, "Who knows? Someday guys – someday." He turned and left for bed.

After he was gone, Irish asked "Do you think you are a piece of crooked iron."

Goldie shook his head, "Iron? I don't know – but crooked, yeah, I think so."

Felix and Marko looked at Goldie slightly different as he and Irish left.

David followed. Marko shook his head, "Felix, do you have it in your head that maybe Goldie and Irish are running like me and you?"

Felix said, "Could be. But why the hell are they staying here?"

* *

A few days later Benny was picking up the mail outside the gate and the big black caddie pulled up.

Benny paid no attention to it and kept gathering the mail – he walked to the gate closed it and locked it.

"Hey Mister is this St. Sebastians?

"Yes, can I help you"?

We wuz wonderin' if you have two guys name of Felix and Marko living with ya."

Benny looked the car over and had suspicions about the occupants. They did not look like uncles and fathers looking for sons and cousins. They looked, to Benny, like Bronx grave diggers looking for a customer.

"Can I tell them whose calling?"

"Just tell them Leo."

"Do you have a last name?"

"Leo is my last name – my first name is Big."

"I'll see if they are available."

The man sitting in the rear called out the window, "If I come in through that gate they will be very available I could assure you."

Benny was skeptical. He was a little afraid. In another time and in another place he would have told the guys that there was no Felix and Marko – a neat lie. But, among other things, the idea of lying was dropping out of his thinking. When he was a good distance from the gate he caught sight of the two of them together and he called, "Felix, Marko there's a guy at the gate wants to see both of you."

Marko dropped the potted plant he was carrying and took a step towards running away but Felix caught him.

Felix asked, "Did they leave a name?"

"Mr Leo – Big Leo."

Marko pulled a little at Felix and tried to break the grasp on him.

107

Felix called, "We'll go see him."

"Okay" said Benny, and he was holding back a smile. It was obvious that the boys knew Big Leo and Marko for sure did not want to see him. "The gate I left locked. Do you want me to open it."

"Naah, We can talk through the bars."

Benny turned and left.

Marko wanted to know if Felix was crazy, "What the hello does he wasn't?"

Felix answered "His truck."

Marko shook his head, "I almost forgot. We left it at the airport."

"I have an idea. Maybe Big Leo will buy it."

They both went to the gate, held the bars with both hands, and wedged their faces between the bars. Together they called

"Hi, Big Leo."

The rear door opened and Big Leo stepped out. He took one look at them and asked "What the hell you guys in for?"

"We're gonna' be monks."

"Maybe,' Leo answered. "If you live long enough."There was quiet for a few moments then Leo growled, "What did you do with my truck."

Marko said, " We left it at Kennedy. I...."

Leo swung at him and hit the gate. He let out a loud hurt sound and grabbed his hand.

"I forgot the keys. Marko reached in his pocket and stuck his hand through the gate bars with the keys dangling from his hand.

Leo swung again and hit the gate again and this time screamed in pain. "The cops did not need keys to drive it away. They just drove it away."

Felix asked, " Can you get it from them?"

Very low and sinister Leo spoke, "The law would like almost 15 grand for the lawful return of the vehicle. Which of course we will not pay but you two clowns have caused me irritation and a very sore hand and I would like very much to embrace you and crush you to death."

"We are very sorry, Big Leo."

"Sorrow is nice but 15 grand is nicer and I intend to charge you what they were going to charge me and I would like to be told how you expect to pay this within 48 hours,"

"We cannot leave here."

"We are becoming Monks."

"I believe you are lying to me – I believe you are on the lam from me and this is the dodge you have taken up to lead me astray. But since I am here you cannot hide any more."

Marko called Leo closer to the gate, "We are here for you, Leo."

"For me?'

"All we got to do is outlive the guys here and we inherit the whole thing as the last surviving members of the order. Just think Leo all that land as far as you can see – yours!"

"What are you talking about?"

Marko explained quietly and confidentially that the rule was the last surviving member of the order would have the right to dispose of the property as he saw fit. There were only a few members and Marko was sure that they could be knocked off in a very short time. "

Just a little time, Leo, that's all we need."

Leo thought this jerk could be right. "Ill give ya a week. Then I will return and Fiddler will have his violin ready to play a concerto if you boys are not making progress."

"Amen, Leo, amen."

Leo got in the car and left.

Felix looked at Marko and announced that "you are crazy."

Marko shrugged his shoulders, "I bought some time."

* *

FOUR EVENINGS LATER

He stopped his car on the side of the Main gate. He climbed over the fence. It was 3 AM and the entire monastery was asleep. He walked down the halls and tip toed down the steps into the kitchen. He could hear the snoring. It sounded like times his high school team would score a touchdown and the crowd roared. It was not quite deafening but loud.

The kitchen was open. He had to find someplace to leave his 'message'. The large soup pot that Ma had left on the stove was still there where she had left it. She was letting the bones soak for hours then boiling them would make the kind of broth that was the secret of all good soups.

He crossed over to the stove and lifted the lid on the soup pot. From his pocket he took the small bag of poison he had taken from Queens and poured it into the soup. He took a ladle and stirred it around so it would not be noticed – replaced the lid - washed the ladle and sneaked up the stairs and out the front door and over the fence to his car.

At 5 AM, Ma came down to the kitchen to begin making breakfast.

She scrambled thirty eggs and put on twenty pieces of toast and started a large pot of coffee. She also boiled some water for the tea drinkers.

Rodney was the next to arrive. He greeted Ma and wished her to have a good day – the he set about his pre-planned duties of making the soup. He went to the refrigerator and took out the chopped vegetables and meat bones to add to the soup. Ma had made the Rodney her exclusive helper and he was loving learning the secrets of home-style cooking. He stirred the ingredients into the soup and set the flame at a boil.

Ma and Rodney set a few places with knives and forks and coffee cups. They began to take out the pieces of toast as they were done and coat each slice with a small amount of butter. Even though some had asked for no butter, Ma said, " a little won't hurt" and so they all got butter.

In the next hour everyone came in and ate breakfast. Ma apologized for 'no orange juice' but resolved to get some for the next day.

After every one left Rodney and Ma cleaned up the dishes and put everything away. Rodney decided to taste the simmering soup.

He took a large soup spoon, blew on it to cool it down and sipped it.

"It tastes delicious so far Ma." And then he fell to the floor. At first Ma didn't see him on the ground and then she heard the groaning and turned around. She ran over to Rodney and bent over him.

"It's been poisoned, Ma."

"Poisoned? So how come you're not dead."

"You forget – I'm an angel. I already died."

"You can't die again?"

"Impossible. But anybody else who drinks that soup will soon go to their reward – which may not be so good - seeing as though they tried to kill everybody here."

111

Ma stepped back and Rodney got off the floor.

"Somebody is trying to ruin us...what could have happened if I had served the soup to everybody," she blessed herself, "it's horrible. I should go tell Albert right away. Oohhh this is horrible>" she was shaking and turning every way in the kitchen. "What will Father Albert say. What will he do to us."

Rodney stopped her, "First, Ma, we did not do this. Someone got in here during the night. We have to find out who did this."

"You are right, Rodney, but how can we tell? We are not detectives."

Rodney asked her if she ever heard of Agatha Christie. She had. "When I was alive I read mysteries by her and I remember one time she let the bad guy think nothing was wrong and they caught him when he was afraid to do what the group did. Sooooo. We will make another soup and serve it at lunch. The person that refuses it will not take any because he believes it to be poisoned."

"Aaahhh then we have him. But what do we do with him?"

Rodney thought for a bit. Then spoke, "We do nothing right away and we keep watching him to find out why he did it?

"Is that dangerous?"

"You and I will watch close and the kitchen will never be untended.

I can sleep here and we can keep it under 24 hour watch.?"

They both looked at each other in silence, then Ma spoke, "Let's make a different soup."

* *

After their encounter with Big Leo, Felix and Marko were very quiet. They were raking the grounds. Not many leaves had fallen yet but Benny wanted to keep the place clean looking. Big Leo was on both their minds – and they were not in a smiling mood.

Marko worked his raking over to Felix and spoke, "Maybe fifteen grand for the car and Big Leo will be happy."

Felix smiled at him, "You think we can pay him fifteen grand and make him happy. How the hell long have you known him? We did him some dirt and he will get even. I would qualify that - he will do better than get even - he will come out on top somehow – someway. And your plan to knock everybody off is not what I would call and admirable plan - it is dangerous. And all the guys around here seem like good guys. "

Marko raked harder and was scraping dirt as he moved away. He was thinking to himself about Albert, Benny, Ma, and the others. He was not ready for that kind of blood bath. He hurried back to Felix.

"Felix, you actually ever do a guy down for the count."

"No, not really."

"You told me you handled the biggest jobs in Queens."

"Yeah, but I didn't murder anybody," he thought a few minutes , "one guy was running away from me and he slipped on a coke bottle and broke his ankle – he was scared - does that count?"

"No – that does not count. Let's take a break and talk."

"Benny will be mad."

"We can tell him we had to pray."

They both dragged their rakes after them and walked away from the main house. They sat on a bench made from logs in a small grove of trees. For a time they were both silent.

The silence was getting to Marko and he spoke up, "What are you thinkin'."

"I'm only thinking of Big Leo and how he could ruin us and get us kicked out of here."

Marko looked at his partner Felix as though he had just lit a 500 pound bomb and was sitting down to watch the fuse, "Are you crazy. Do you want to stay here? I can't believe it. No liquor – no women – no action ---

"I get out of here and there's no women – some liquor – no action – the difference is minimal. And on the other hand no landlord hasslin' ya' and meals are all cooked and the air is fresh not mixed with them poison gasses. I kinda' like it here."

"Felix it's almost time for lunch. Let's go before you have me believing every thing I hear."

* *

Lunch was all ready. Ma and Rodney had set all the places with napkins, soup spoons, and a knife and fork. Rodney (who could not be seen by anyone except Ma) whispered in the corner, " It's all set whoever rejects the soup is the guilty party."

Benny led them in grace before meals and then they all started eating. Goldie reached for bread and buttered it with an inch or so of butter, Marko blew on his soup and remarked it was a little hot, Felix crunched some crackers on top of it, Irish got up and headed toward the kitchen.

"It's Irish Ma, He's not taking the soup."

"I don't believe it Rodney, he's such a nice lad. And he's helpful in the kitchen."

Just then he reappeared carrying a dish of grated cheese. He smiled at Ma and said " I love a little cheese on the soup." He sat down and started on the soup.

Rodney looked at Ma, "It's not him."

"But who is it Rodney? They're all eating the soup and even helping themselves to more."

"I know the original soup was poisoned."

Ma and Rodney observed them all drinking the soup and smiling about how good it was. They had some cookies for desert, then Benny stood up and announced, "prayer and class will start in twenty minutes and all of you will be there."

They all left and Rodney sat on one of the empty chairs and Ma sat next to him. Rodney supported is head with his hand, leaned forward to Ma and spoke, "We have a problem."

* *

During class Goldie and Marko got into a bit of a shouting match over the story of Zaccheus the tax collector. Goldie thought it was nice of Zaccheus to give half of everything he owned to the poor. Marko said he didn't see how you could give half of everything. Goldie said that Jesus would be lucky to get 20 bucks out of a guy like Marko. Marko argued that he gave 50 bucks to the church at Christmas. Goldie said he gave three $400 suits to the missions.

Marko said you probably lifted them and they didn't fit. Goldie told Marko to shut up and or he would be 'shut up' by Goldie. They both stood and Benny spied the outline of a gun when Goldie reached under his robe.

Benny jumped between them and told them to relax. Father Albert spoke loudly that the next time any outburst came in class or anywhere on monastery grounds they would promptly be dismissed and forced to leave. "Such conduct is not what makes a brother at St. Sebastian's and it never will – so to continue with that sort of explosive outbursts it is better that it be nipped in the bud and the perpetrators forced to leave."

Father Albert left the class. He told Benny to lead them in act of forgiveness prayer and send them to their chores.

Everyone started to rise. Benny told them "remain seated."

"Brothers, I think we have a problem. I believe when the argument between Goldie and Marko heated up I spotted the outline of a gun beneath Goldie's robe. Not only did I see that outline but I saw several of you reach under your robes maybe to get prayer beads or maybe to get something else."

He paused and looked around the class. Everyone was silent. "I will not talk about this again, but tonight I will place a basket outside my door and anyone of you that may by some strange odd set of circumstances have a gun in your possession will place the weapon in the box - no questions asked. But there is no holding back. I want all the guns you gentlemen have in that box by morning."

He looked around the room in silence. His head moved to each of them – some looked away and could not face Benny. When he had looked them all down, he said, "Close your eyes. Lord we thank you for the life we are trying to live at St. Sebastians, Forgive us if sometimes we seem to be doing the wrong thing – but we are trying and give us the energy to rid ourselves of any encumbrances - like guns – that we may have. Amen." You are all dismissed.

* *

"There are ways to rid yourself of certain peoples without guns," Irish was talking to Goldie after they the class.

"Ssshhh not so loud we don't want the walls around this place to hear that we may have guns."

"But we do have guns, Goldie, makes no difference."

"Are you turning your weapon in, Irish."

"Who knows, Benny was really pissed, if he don't get some guns he is gonna' really blow his top."

On another path leading away from the main house, Marko was in deep conversation with Felix.

"This is a major change, Felix, we can no longer just pop these guys off one at a time – it is going to be sneaky."

"Like how would you suggest, Marko."

"Drowning is a favorite but nobody ever goes near the river and you can wade in that pond."

"How did you know about the pond."

"I walked through it chasing a butterfly."

"Chasin' a butterfly? Since when do you start collectin' butterflys."

"It was pretty, but I didn't catch it."

They were both silent as they walked.

Marko finally spoke up, "If only Benny hadn't seen your gun."

Felix nodded his head slowly, "Yeah, if only?" He thought a few seconds, "You mean your gun, Marko. Mine is in the place I sleep."

Marko stopped walking he thought for a few seconds, "Your gun is not with you."

"Nah – it's too heavy to pull around all day."

Marko shook his head more, "I ain't got my gun and you ain't got your gun – and Benny saw the outline of a gun – that means somebody else has got guns around here."

Felix's mouth formed a circle as he slowly said "Wow. That could be dangerous."

We've got to be careful...I am thinking those two gentlemen by name of Goldie and Irish may be set on carrying out a task not unlike our own."

* *

"What the hell do you carry a gun around for...this is not Queens this is .... Is.....what do you call it?"

Goldie backed into a corner and Irish said, "I think I heard them call it a monastree..."

"We could have had a lot of trouble....we could have been exposed and then where the heck would we be...."

"We could always stay here, Goldie."

"Stay here – why do you want to stay here..."

"We got a bed and three meals a day...that's a lot."

"But we got no freedom."

"We got more freedom than if we get caught. Then we do time in jail or worse."

Irish had Goldie in a corner in back of the garages and was letting him know in no uncertain terms that carrying a gun around was not a very good idea. Even thought he knew that Goldie had to carry a gun and he did too, but not to class where it could be exposed.

They both finally agreed that yelling wasn't solving the problem and they would confines their artillery to a discreet hiding place in their rooms.

* *

That evening the box outside Benny' room contained 18 guns of several different makes. He stashed them in his room. He would turn them into garbage soon as he found the proper time.

* *

ANGELS 'OFFICES' IN QUEENS

In back of the hardware store a meeting was in progress. Angel sat at the head of the table. He was surrounded by the 'book', his accountant, the 'bag', his lawyer, and his body guard Freddie.

Hans Hubrick, an architect, and his lovely assistant Claudia, who happened to be Angel's niece, had their drawings spread out on the table.

Hubrick was speaking, " And Mr Angel, depending on the land available, we may be able to construct more than 500 houses, three parks, a recreation building, four stores selling various necessities, and a school. It will be a neat little town."

Claudia smiled and twisted her body to face Angel, "Aunt Clara, says to say hello."

Angel's face switched from a smiling orange color to a prune. He still did not like the idea of any family involved in his business but somebody got word to his mother, who got word to Aunt Clara, who knew an architect who lived three houses down and always smiled at her when she was taking out her garbage. Angel thought, 'that was not a first class connection' and his face shriveled more. Hans and Claudia were talking up a storm about the plans and Angel interrupted with two words, "How much?"

Hans stopped, "How much what?"

"It gonna' cost.?"

"That's hard to say."

"Just think about it and come up with a number - now"

"I really really can't."

"If you don't come up with a number then you think I got to be crazy to sit and listen to all this stuff and maybe it ain't real."

Claudia slinked again, "Clara said you had plenty of...."

"You mean my aunt Clara who I saw once 12 years ago...."

"Yes I believe so – a lovely woman."

" You can call her lovely but I can think of other names."

"...money. Anyway, she said you have plenty of money. And this would be a good legitimate business for you to get in."

119

"I am in a legitimate business."

"Aunt Clara said you are just kind of racketeering – not really legitimate."

"I own a hardware store – a very legitimate enterprise. And you can tell our Aunt Clara that playing footsie with this guy drawing pictures is not exactly the most legitimate thing in the world – I can smell it."

Hans jerked his head up – he would defend himself against this slander, "Are you saying that I am not on the up and up I am just trying to help you – free of charge – since you are becoming owner of a large tract of land."

Angel stared at himm "Where in the hell did you hear I was coming into a large tract of land – which I might add I have not come into as yet."

"Aunt Clara."

Angel, sat back, hit his head, "Where in hell did I get these damn relatives?" He stared at the layout of papers on the table then m0oved his eyes to Hans and the voluptuous Claudia, shook his head and said "Get out.

Claudia started, "But uncle Angel...

"Get out." He turned to his two workers, "help them get out – now!

The workers jumped in put all the papers together and hustled them out the door. Angel sat alone. He was thinking about Irish and Goldie. He finally called "Hubert."

Hubert, the giant, opened the door, "What yas' want Mr. Angel.?"

"Have we heard from Goldie and Irish?"

"Nothin."

"Call Fiddler - We're paying them a visit."

* *

In a motel down the road from the monastery, Fiddler was talking to Big Leo on the phone:

Fiddler: I am in a motel near those guys.

Big Leo: Have you made a move?

Fiddler: I did the soup like you told me and they all should have been in heaven by now. I don't know what happened.

Big Leo: Fiddler, I do not like excuses.

Fiddler: I am telling you that soup had enough tomato-flavored arsenic in to take out the third army.

Big Leo: We are not interested in the third army or the fourth – we are interested in a couple of monks – is that clear?

Fiddler: I understand, Big Leo.

Big Leo: I'll talk to you in a couple of days. I have to take my wife to Atlantic City. She goes crazy on those penny machines. – Goodnight.

They hung up. Fiddler was thinking of bombs. He thought he could set a series of bombs throughout the grounds and then set them off on occasion and one by one the monks would go down. He turned on the television and watched another episode of Law and Order. He liked the show but he was convinced that "one of these days they will not get their man."

* *

All the brothers were gathered for the evening meal, Father Albert stood up, "I have some sad news to tell you. Father Timmons my closest priest friend for many, many years has died. He has always had a special love for St. Sebastians and before he died he asked to be buried here. Some of you may not know it but

121

the long path on the south side of the main building leads to a small cemetery where several priests of the order have been put to rest. Tomorrow you will take turns digging his grave and the funeral will take place in two days. On that day we will have many visitors and all of us must be aware of being on our best behavior. We will celebrate the mass of the resurrection at ten o'clock on the day of the funeral. We will all attend. Father Timmons was a genuine and real friend of St Sebastian's and we will see that he is properly cared for in his last rites." Albert sat down.

All ate the meal in relative silence.

Benny was thinking that the guys seemed to be taking Father Timmons' death to heart – they were all calm. No major disruptions.

Could the whole idea of these jokers actually becoming good religious brothers and maybe even priests someday be somehow catching on. It would be too much to hope for but like Albert always says God acts in ways that are unusual - not the norm.

MO was thinking – what an impending disaster! He was trying to visualize people coming to church for the funeral and run into the brothers Goldie, Marko, Irish, and Felix. He hadn't figured out what they were doing here yet. He remembered talking to Goldie, after Izzy's wake, about Benny and the need for priests at St. Sebastian's.

He could not believe that was the reason he had joined. It was strange.

Dave thought about Felix. He knew he was Baby's little brother and he had explained to Baby about the priest shortage at St. Sebastians – could she have told him and he decided to join – he didn't think so. Baby had explained her brother as living from one scheme to the next – was this another scheme?

They all finished their meal and left.

* *

The next day Felix and Marko were in the Monastery's graveyard digging. They had been working for about an hour and the hole was not very deep.

"Benny says we have to go down six feet and we ain't down a foot yet."

"That is the law, Marko."

"I think one foot down would be enough...I remember two guys that I was..."

"I don't want to hear it Marko – you could have covered them with grass seed but we ain't doin' that here."

"I was just mentionin'..."

Felix stopped him..."No more talk Marko – dig"

They dug for a short time. Felix was thinking that maybe a hole in the ground would be a good place to get rid of some of the bodies that he and Marko were under orders to produce. He figgered Father Albert, Benny, Goldie and Irish. He thought the rest of the people would just leave – maybe Dave would want to stay and he sure hoped that MO left.

Dave appeared and sat down on a pile of dirt near the hole.

"Mind if I watch?"

Felix stopped digging and looked at him, "You want to watch us dig. It's just a hole."

"Aaah my friends – more than a hole. A doorway to eternity."

"To us it is a hole."

"Big enough for a casket."

Dave continued, "Alas, poor Father Timmons, How did he leave this mortal coil/"

Felix, looked at Dave and wondered if the guy ever talked normal, "he had a heart attack."

* *

Rodney looked at Ma in amazement, "You did what?"

"I invited two girls, lovely girls, Debra and Linda, from the neighborhood, to spend as few days with us."

"You can't do that."

"Why not."

"They're girls, women., whatever. They can't stay here."

"I know they can't become priests, but they'll just stay for a few days and they can do a lot of major cleaning around here – these boys do not know how to clean."

"But we have to teach the boys, or novices or whatever, to clean, they can't have maids."

"These girls are not maids. But they are hard workers and when they see the condition of the rooms around here they'll straighten them out in no time."

"Albert will not permit it."

"He doesn't have to know."

"But...but..."

"When they arrive...we'll see what happens."

* *

That night Fiddler left his motel carrying two heavy suitcases and a shovel. His plan was to sneak onto the monastery property and place a series of small booby traps around the grounds. He had gotten the small traps, called poppers, from one of Big Leo's clients. They were simple just attach one wire to a screw and go away. He had tried one out in the Motel parking lot and there was no trouble at all.

The Motel manager had complained of the noise and he denied knowing anything about it. The popper had left a big hole in the blacktop but the manager never noticed it.

He would control them with his cell phone and he would be able to set off a series of explosions hopefully getting rid of some of the residents. He had talked to Big Leo before he took his wife to Atlantic City and he promised to have good news for him by the time he returned. He drove his car about a half mile pass the main entrance to St Sebastian – there was an old road there and he could pull the car in and keep it hidden till morning.

He got out of the car – he could see the lights from the main building – it did not seem far. He tied the shovel to one of the suitcases and he started into the St. Sebastian grounds. He had to go through heavy brush and he was mad that he had not got himself a big knife to cut through the growth. His plan would be to plant a popper in the main entrance driveway and several in the gardens...he knew he couldn't get them all done tonight but at least he could get started.

He was getting closer now – the brush was thinning out.

CRASH – BANG – OUCH he was falling down he landed smack on the ground. He was groggy and a scared. He looked around and felt around. He could feel dirt on all sides and dirt on the bottom – he was in a big oblong hole – he was in a hole shaped like a grave.

He had held onto the two bags but he didn't have the shovel. He tried jumping to the top but he couldn't reach it. The sides of the hole were moist and slippery he kept sliding back. He didn't want to step on his bag full of poppers because they might pop with the pressure on them. He just kept trying to dig a foothold in the sides but nothing would take. He tried again and again. He kept trying for more than two hours. He was trapped. He was exhausted. He collapsed after one last leap – his head fell to his chest and he was asleep.

* *

The next morning visitors started arriving about 8:00 for Father Timmon's 8:30 funeral. Felix and Marko were directing traffic and getting cars parked in an orderly fashion. Dave was standing by the door directing people to the chapel. Goldie and Irish were handing out prayer and song sheets that Albert had printed in the village.

MO and Benny were altar boys. Most of the guests were middle to old age couples who had known Father Timmons for a long time.

But among the guests were two young women carrying luggage. When Ma spotted them she rushed to their side and led them to seats at the side of the chapel. They were Debra and Linda. After they were seated they started to speak to Ma but she put her finger to her lips – they became quiet. Then Ma whispered, "after the service we'll talk."

The funeral director arrived with Father Timmons and he was brought into the chapel as a record of "On Eagles Wings" played.

Albert, Benny, and MO greeted the casket and the service was under way.

Outside Felix and Marko gave each other a high five for getting all the cars parked so they could get out. Marko had called upon his skill as a 'parker' learned from worker at an old Kinney parking lot in Manhattan. Felix had parked cars at Yankee stadium.

"We have about an hour before they come out," Marko said.

"That gives us time to check on the grave."

"What do we have to check on it for – it's a grave."

"Make sure we didn't leave anything hanging around loose."

They started walking to the grave site.

"You know, Felix, we didn't do bad. Working on the funeral I actually felt good.'

"Yeah, I know what you mean - something good and something useful. I ain't done that in a long time."

"Me neither."

They were silent for a time.

Felix looked at Marko opened his mouth to speak then stopped - shook his head "no" and continued walking. Something inside wanted him to talk about their lives changing at St. Sebastian's but it wouldn't come out.

"Hey, Felix, look at the grave, I can see a shovel we left out."

"Marko, that ain't our shovel."

Marko picked up the shovel, "It doesn't look like ours."

Felix was at the edge of the grave and looking down, "C'mere Marko."

Marko went to the edge and looked over at the sleeping Fiddler.

They both looked down at him for a few beats then Marko shouted down, "Fiddler, you got to get out of there. We got to put a casket

In there."

Fiddler stirred. He was groggy and shaky. He woke and looked up at Marko and Felix, "Where am I?"

"You're in our grave."

"Am I dead."

"No. You're just in our grave."

"Get me the hell out – it feels awful spooky."

Marko lowered the shovel, "Grab this."

Felix said," The grave is for Father Timmons – the service is almost over and he'll be brought here."

Fiddler grabbed hold of the shovel and they started pulling him up.

"Hey wait a minute my bags – I got to have them."

Marko said, "The people are coming out of church are they important?"

"Put me down. I have to get them."

"Jeez. Hurry, Fiddler – They'll be here in a minute."

Fiddler let go of the shovel – dropped back into the grave - grabbed both bags – he held one up and it nearly reached the top, "Grab this Marko, and be careful – don't bang it against anything." Marko lie down and reached into the grave – grabbed the handle and pulled it out.

"Get this one Marko." They got the second one up the same way.

Felix started pulling up Fiddler, but suddenly Benny's voice, "What's going on Felix."

Benny and MO were leading the procession of mourners.

Marko answered, "We had a visitor last night and he fell in the grave."

MO asked, "Those are his bags?"

Felix answered, "Yeah, I guess he was going to stay awhile."

Benny said, "Get him out quick or he'll be covered with dirt."

Felix pulled Fiddler up.

MO looked at him, "Fiddler? Big Leo's guy."

"Hi, MO."

The procession bearing the casket on rollers arrived.

"Marko, Felix take the guy and his luggage into the house – I'll talk to him later, "then Benny struck a prayerful pose and turned to greet the procession bearing the casket.

* *

Felix and Marko carrying Fiddlers luggage rushed him away, just as the funeral procession arrived.

The next day Fiddler was sent on his way. He explained his presence to Benny as looking for rabbits to hunt and he fell in the open grave. Felix and Marko knew the reason to be different but they were too frightened to open their mouths.

Benny had to admit that it was not a very good excuse but he let it go.

* *

Rodney opened the door ajar and peeked in - Ma was working with the girls, Linda and Debra. He slipped in and tapped Ma on the shoulder- she was about to say something when he quickly put his finger to her lips, then beckoned her to come to another part of the kitchen behind the freezers. Ma nodded okay and turned to the girls, " I'll be over there but you can keep peeling the carrots and potatoes,"

Linda asked, "When do we meet the boys?'

Ma turned to her, " I told you that you would meet them at lunch, not before."

Debra shook her head, " I can peel potatoes at home you told us there was a lot of nice men we could meet here."

"You will. You will."

Ma slipped behind the freezer and Rodney greeted her with "They will not."

"Rodney, I think they'll be nice for the boys to meet."

"Ma, you must listen to me. Women are not allowed to be residents of St. Sebastians. This is a men's monastery. We don't have accommodations for women."

"I'm a woman."

"I know that but you're different. Those girls are very attractive they could easily be a temptation for the men to forget about the idea of keeping celibate and they could have a tryst."

"A tryst?"

From the part of the kitchen where the girls were the sound of Benny's voice came, "Ma" then he spotted the two girls "Linda – Debra - what are you doing here?"

"Ma invited us."

Benny recognized the two girls from the old neighborhood. They were two of the girls that he and MO had dated and were often held up by Ma as great wife potential. He had gone out with Debra several times and they had come close to having a sexual good time but they never got over the final hump – so to speak. She was good looking and her father was a cop and her mother worked in the library. A nice catch but Benny was not on that marriage track anymore. Linda had been close to MO and he never did know how close they came to finalizing their relationship but MO was here now and he would not be thinking of marriage – at least he did not think so.

Ma came back from the freezer, "Benny isn't it nice that the girls are here."

"Yes, Ma, but you know they can only visit not stay."

"They would be a big help for morale. I think you boys could use a couple of nice girls to brighten things up."

"They would certainly brighten things up."

Albert came into the kitchen. He stopped and apologized

for interrupting.

Ma spoke, "This is Father Albert, girls. He is a priest. Sometimes he acts strict but you'll get used to him."

Albert sat down and shook his head, "Benny what is going on here?"

He started to answer but Ma took over, "Albert, the girls are old friends from the neighborhood – they are lovely people – and I invited them here to cheer the boys up."

Albert shook his head, "Cheer the boys up."

Benny thought Albert would faint but he quickly spoke, "they are just here for a short – very short – visit."

"But Ma said to bring plenty of clothes, actually I took just about all my clothes, Ma said there was lots to do here, and we would be meeting some nice guys."

"That's what I said, Debra."

Albert stood up slowly, " actually we have no room here for..."

Linda piped up, " There was plenty of room on the third floor Ma moved us in and we have very pleasant accommodations."

"The third floor..."

"Away from the boys – we have our own bathroom and everything."

Albert turned to Ma, "How long have these young ladies been here."

"They arrived during Father Timmons' funeral."

"They're all moved in...on the third floor."

Albert shook his head, "they will have to leave as soon as possible."

"They have to meet all the boys first."

"Meet the boys? First? Ma, this is a monastery, if the world ever finds out we have two pretty young women mixed in with ....the rest of us, we will be slaughtered by the press and the radio and the cardinal."

"They are harmless."

Benny shook his head and looked at his mother, " Ma, these men are

Learning to live without women, " he looked at her and shook his head, "women their own age. They might want to engage these girls in...

Albert, over the shock, and now in control again spoke up "Sex, Ma, sex. The risk of having these beautiful girls around is not a good idea. Benny, get them some Monk robes and keep them under cover, ,I don't want the men to meet them, until they can leave, which has to be soon," He turned and left the kitchen.

Benny nodded agreement, "Alright girls put down the potatoes and carrots and follow me."

Debra and Linda looked at Ma.

Ma nodded they should go with Benny. As the left she called after them, "No trysting..." then in small voice to herself, "whatever that is."

* *

LEO'S OFFICE

"You fell in a grave! How did you fall in a grave? If you don't tell me something that makes sense you would be better if you had stayed in the grave."

Fiddler was sure Big Leo meant it. He began to think maybe he should have stayed at St. Sebastian's – the food was good – the beds couldn't be that bad – the countryside was real pretty. He recalled a time about four years ago when he went into a church over in Brooklyn and this minister was giving everybody, and there were hundreds, hell, or holy hell, for sinning. He screamed Jesus will not condemn you – he will forgive and forget – just go and sin no more.

Then he stopped screaming and said quietly Lord keep my focus on you and stop sin from ruling my life....Then he stopped – the whole church was all silent. Fiddler got scared he was there to punish, Iggie, a cheater, for Big Leo, but the quiet was very very quiet – nobody in that church moved – the minister in a low low voice said I hear your voice Jesus, I hear you, we all hear you, and you are telling us to be good - to not sin- to not misbehave... then the

Singers, all dressed in blue with white angel wings, started singing and clapping a song -

> No one to walk with,
> But I'm happy in the pew
> Ain't misbehavin',
> I'm savin' my love for you
> I know for certain,
> The one I love,
> I through with sinin',
> It's just him I'm thinkin' of
> I'm savin' my love for him
> Ain't misbehavin',
> I'm savin' my love for
> JESUS

Then the preacher screamed "what are we ain't doin" and the whole group of people there screamed all at once WE AIN'T MISBEHAVIN' NO MORE...

Everybody started leaving and he couldn't spot Iggie. One of the dumbos with Fiddler finally spotted Iggie and he was dressed like a singing angel. Fiddler called the boys off and Iggie escaped for another day.

"Speak, Fiddler, or else!" Big Leo was screaming at Fiddler. His voice sounded a lot like that preacher in Brooklyn but the message was a lot different."

"Big Leo, I had all the poppers in the bag. I was goin' to plant them all around where these guys walk and one by one they would be 'popped' off. I was sneaking in the grounds at night and BANG I fell in a grave that was dug that day, and not there the day before, and I got knocked out. Felix and Marko found me the next day. I saved the poppers, Nobody knew why I was there so I can return and get the job done. I never misbehaved. That's good – isn't it Leo?"

Leo looked at him and finally spoke, "It is so stupid that I believe you."

Then it got very quiet. Fiddler was thinking of the Brooklyn church again and in some strange way Big Leo was the minister about to give a loud, fiery, order. Finally he spoke, I am going there with you, Fiddler, we are ending this thing one way or the other." He pulled out of his pocket a little address book, the kind companies give away in December every year, and he turned pages. "We will go there in three days when my wife goes to Atlantic City again."

* *

ST. SEBASTIANS

Albert and Benny sat in Albert's private office with Debra and Linda. The girls were dressed in monk's robes and the hood (?) drawn over their heads. The loose hanging robe kept the girl's bodies covered and it was impossible to tell their sex.

For the past three days the girls had been slipping into the men's rooms after they left and made the beds and kept the dust at a minimum. When the kitchen was clear they had helped Ma in all her food preparation. Albert remarked on how they had performed admirably but they were women and this was a man's monastery. He explained the Church's strong position on keeping women from joining monasteries. Albert instructed Benny to get to work immediately on helping the girls get home and away from St. Sebastians.

* *

ANGELS OFFICE

Angel was getting more and more upset. He couldn't get rid of the damn architect. Claudia, the architects' assistant, had cried to Aunt Clara, who immediately called his mother, who called him and told him that Uncle Phil, Clara's deceased husband, had been the best friend of his father and his father had gotten the money from Uncle Phil to open the candy store. Which all added up to Angel 'owed" aunt Clara 'cause without her there would have been no candy store.

So he agreed to have another meet with Hans, the architect.

Hans had all his drawings laid out on the desk. He was talking about a main artery from which several streets would branch off. It reminded Angel of a Christmas tree. He kept talking about a library for the young children and another library for the adults. Angel had been to two libraries in his life and both of them had kids in them. He never knew there were two kinds of libraries. Hans was suggesting that he could get Macy's and the A&P to open stores on one of the Christmas Tree branches.

Angel had never done too well in Math at school. He could remember trying to divide one fifth into one fourth and as far as he could tell it was impossible. In his business he could add and subtract and once in a while divide. He knew what 5 to 2 paid and even 7 to 3. He knew a lot of basic math and he also knew that you could not build the kind of thing Hans was talking about without spending 'zillions' of dollars. Hans had to be hustling because if he looked around Angel's office located behind the candy story he could see – walls that had never been painted, plaster coming off the ceiling, orange crates for chairs, and a table made from two carpenter's horses and a door, that didn't fit the closet, for the desk top.

Cousin Claudia kept smiling and getting erasers for Hans as he made adjustments in the drawings spread out on the desk. Every time Angel tried to get a figure of what it would cost Claudia would quickly up and tell Hans not to worry about the money, "Aunt Clara said Uncle Angel could afford it easily."

So they just kept drawing pictures on the drawings and smiling and Claudia kept nudging Hans in the ribs and he would smile and Angel would sigh and ask again "What the hell is it going to cost?" He figured that maybe all this nonsense would come to a screeching end when Angel proved to them that he did not have the two zillion dollars or whatever.

Angel was fighting to keep awake as the two of them kept tickling each other with more grand ideas. He nodded off and then was suddenly awakened with "...how about tomorrow, Uncle Angel?"

"Tomorrow for what?"

"All of us visit the site," Claudia answered.

Hans smiled at Angel and said in glowing terms, "Yes, that would be wonderful – it would help me move my creative juices further up this painful road."

"You poor boy are you in pain?" He sighed and took Claudia's hand – then gently nodded his head.

Angel could not believe this was all happening. He was trying to steal some land by knocking off a couple of monks and his Aunt had already assumed he had the land and he had money and he was going to build a Tinker Toy town so a guy named Hans could keep pinching his niece Claudia. This is a crazy nutty scene – but he didn't know how to get out of it. But maybe if Mr. Hans could look at the land he might not think a Christmas tree plan would work and the whole thing would be over. Over, except for Goldie and Irish, knocking off the principals and getting the land to Angel who would promptly turn it over to a bank for cash.

"Be here at nine and we will visit the site."

They smiled and seemed happy.

"Bring a lunch," Angel said and got up from his desk and went to the stairs to go to his apartment. He had to lie down and try to get rid of his headache.

* *

THE CARDINAL'S OFFICE

In the Fifth avenue office of the Cardinal, Harold, the Cardinal's secretary, reread the letter for the third time. He finally made up his mind. He would go into the Cardinal's office and show him this letter. The Cardinal may end up a little angry but on the whole Gregory thought it was better that he see it.

The Cardinal looked up, "Yes, Harold ?"

"Excellency. This letter was received in the morning mail and I think you might find it interesting."

"Some one needs prayers? Tell them fine I..."

"No, Excellency, it's a bit different."

" Read it to me."

"First, it is sent to you by Mrs Benny, from St Sebastians...

"Is that the place in Haverstraw that is complaining that they may be closed?'

"No, Excellency that is St Andrew's - this is the place upstate that the advertising man came to talk to us about – remember?"

"Not really. Go on."

137

"Dear Excellency, I pray for you with all your problems. Being the head of the New York Diocese must be a big job. I used to live in Brooklyn and have they got problems! Anyway the important thing is St. Sebastian. My son, Benny, joined the order and according to Father Albert he may become a priest someday. I think that would be good but I am not sure of his brother, MO, who came up here too and joined. After both my boys joined I decided to join too. I came and started doing the cooking. I am getting along great and the boys seems to enjoy the meals. But we really need help in doing the other work of the monastery – you know laundry and making beds and keeping the place neat and clean. I decided to get two lovely young girls from the old neighborhood to get their tails up her and give us a hand. When they heard there were men here they came but as soon as they got here I made perfectly clear that these men were not to be touched. They are here now and doing very well. They stay away from the men, and Albert keeps the men away from them – but Albert said he can not let the women (the young ones that came to help me) live in the monastery. We have hundreds of room with nobody in them and he won't let them stay.

I am writing to you to simply tell Fr. Albert that the girls can stay as long as they keep their distance – so to speak. I am sure you agree with me so just drop a line to Fr. Albert that it will be no problem for Debra and Linda to stay with us – thanking you in advance and I hope you get the rest of the diocese straightened out. Signed

Sincerely, Ma, Cook."

The Cardinal was silent. He kept shaking his head – then " what the heck can happen next – she simply wants a ...."

"Debra and Linda."

"....Debra and Linda to live in the monastery. Even though I am sure she is right when she says they have a hundred empty rooms."

"How shall I answer her, excellency?"

"We will visit her

* *

ST. SEBASTIANS

Albert asked Benny to stop for a quiet chat after dinner – he was on his way to his office now. Benny had lots of idea that he knew needed talking about and he hoped Albert had some of the same ideas. Albert's office was on the ground floor of the main building and Benny had only been in it once in all the time he had been at St Sebastians.

Albert saw him through the open door of his office and beckoned him in. He entered and sat in the chair opposite Albert's desk. The office was very simple a square wooden desk, three chairs, two bookcases, a crucifix and on the wall several group pictures of the early years of St. Sebastians.

Albert, after a few pleasantries, cut to the chase. "I'm concerned about a few of our members. I've been working on a few ideas and thoughts that I feel we should talk about."

Benny nodded in agreement. "I understand."

"I sincerely feel that Goldie, Irish, Felix, and Marko should be asked to leave. In my mind they just do not seem like they will ever be able to receive Holy Orders for the priesthood. Their presence here is a mystery to me. They act at times like hoodlums anxious to get to another level of 'hoodlumese'. They do not act like novitiates that I am accustomed to. Now you are closer to them. Let me ask you what you think? Do you ever see them in prayer? Do they study our lessons? Do they seem to grow in the spiritual life in any way?"

Benny wanted to agree 100% with Albert and see these four sent packing before breakfast. But he sensed a tinge of something he found hard to explain that made him 'want to save them from being sent packing. He could see each of them finding themselves in a new way. They were hoodlums – he knew that. But couldn't they come around and reform and help St. Sebastians. Sending them off would just condemn them back to the streets and they would continue to be petty criminals. Just yesterday his brother MO had told him that all four of the guys mentioned were drifters around Queens and worked for two Bosses, Big Leo and Angel. They worked by collecting gambling money and pushing people around that Angel and Big Leo decided needed pushing around. MO even told him that Fiddler the guy they rescued from the grave was a 'gun' for Big Leo. Benny knew all this but he knew that maybe some of the good around St. Sebastians would rub off on them.

"Albert, I think, you're right. They are not priest material, but they could become believers and faithful workers. I want to keep them for a while longer and I will explain to them they are out of the Theology classes for the time being."

"I have a great faith in you, Benny. We will keep them for a while longer. And your brother, MO, and Dave – maybe there's hope for them. We'll see."

* *

"Have you got all of yours planted?"

"I got them all set Marko. When some unsuspecting innocent person walks by one of the tulip bulbs I planted – it can be their last walk. Boom they go in a blaze of Tulip seeds."

"And mine are in the ground, too. Let me see your map Felix."

"What map?"

"You were supposed to make a map of every place you put one of the 'poppers' so we could know when to 'pop' them."

Felix was silent. He said nothing for thirty seconds.

Marko spoke very quietly, "You didn't make a map?" Silence

"How, Felix, my idiotic friend are we supposed to know where they are so we can make sure they will get somebody when they pop and assist us in fulfilling our mission to acquire these lovely premises for us – the survivors."

Silence.

"Do you remember Fiddler telling us that on this little key pad which you have and I have are numbers...the poppers with the same number will "pop" when I push the button." He pushed the button.

"BOOM" and dirt about 25 feet away went into the air.

Ma rushed out of the kitchen, "What was that?"

The girls were right behind her. "It sounded like a small cannon," Linda said.

"More like a truck back firing," said Diane

"Did you see a truck go be here, Felix?' Ma asked.

"No, Ma, trucks don't go by here in the back of the building."

"Well, you boys stop playing with fireworks or whatever it was.'

She turned and left followed by the two girls.

"Well, now we have a mess – a genuine mess."

"Maybe I can name the spots where ..."

"You can try...but you can't remember your name."

"Yes, I can."

* *

Goldie and Irish were stacking wood on the other side of the building from Marko and Felix.

"You hear that, Goldie."

"Sounded like a baby bomb."

"You know, Goldie, those two 'dips' Felix and Marko I bet are responsible."

The two stopped stacking wood and sat for a few seconds staring at each other. Finally Irish spoke, "Goldie, I'm thinking Felix and Marko might be here for the same reason we are here."

"You mean knock everybody off so they can own this place."

"That's what I mean."

"They can't do it – this is our gig – we got to get it for Angel or he will drop us in a big hole someplace."

"The trouble is nobody wants to pull a trigger. We keep trying to figure out a way to do the deed but nothing is happening."

"We got to get on with it...no more excuses."

They are quiet for a few minutes.

Finally Irish spoke – "I'm not sure I can do it."

"Do what?"

"Shoot these nice people."

Goldie looked at him for a few seconds. He was saying what Goldie was thinking. How could they put a gun in Albert's mouth or even Benny who was always trying to help him. He knew he couldn't do it to Mom – He was not going to kill a cook like her.

* *

Every day since he had come to St. Sebastians Benny spent about thirty minutes after breakfast (or sometimes before breakfast) in their little chapel praying. Albert was usually there saying an 'office' – which was a group of prayer said daily by most religious people. Albert gave Benny a book with the office in it and told Benny to try it. Benny had read it faithfully for about ten days then gave it up. The prayers were too difficult for him. He knew what they said but they seemed to leave out his problems or his reasons to pray. He talked to Albert about it and Albert told him to put aside for a while and maybe he would come back to them.

That was happening. He was reading the office these days and enjoying the prayers. The change had a lot to do with his discussions about prayer with Albert. In the words of Albert you did not have to take all the prayers literally – you used the prayers to place your spirit in a place close to God then you could spring off from that...bring the prayers to more of a shape and reality to suit your needs – do this and it praised God just as much and more than following the prayers literally. Benny always let his mind drift to needs he saw in the world and how God could help those in need. Now as the words of the office were read in his mind he could feel the needs of St Sebastian's growing and how it needed help. Other thoughts drifted through his mind and he really felt the words of the 'office' were helping him direct attention to an array of worldly and spiritual needs.

Today his prayers were on his companions at Sebastians. He knew, as Albert, did that Goldie and Irish and Felix and Marko were not 'into' their 'vocations' as much as they could be. He liked those guys and he prayed for them – he kept asking God to help him find the right place for them. Then a mini-miracle happened Goldie and Irish slipped in the back of the chapel and were sitting there quietly.

Benny could hardly control himself from getting up and sitting with them – but he knew it was wrong and he would wait to speak to them later.

He returned to reading the office. When he finished the boys were still there. He made up his mind to speak to them. He would just say hello and if they felt like talking they would start something.

He blessed himself, slipped his prayer book onto the shelf beneath the seat, got up, genuflected and walked to the back of the church.

"Hi guys," he said as he approached them.

They looked at each other, then Goldie turned and spoke, "Benny can we talk to you."

"Sure, Goldie."

Irish spoke up, " we'd like to speak right here. The Church makes it easier for us to say what we want to say."

"Nobody's here so go ahead. God won't mind a little conversation – He hears a lot of it all day."

Irish nudged Goldie in the ribs, " Go ahead Goldie, you're on."

So Goldie talked. He told Benny how he and Irish worked for a man named Angel, "And he is no angel." And they got into a lot of debt with him. So much debt that Angel was in the mood to knock both of us "off."

"Kill you?"

Irish nodded, "In Angel's world owing money is a serious sin and the punishment can be very severe...very severe."

Goldie went on. We heard about this place, St.Sebastians, was taking a dive for lack of priests. And we further heard that the last remaining members of the organization would inherit the whole place. So we told Mr. Angel that we would join the outfit and be the last surviving members.

Benny asked, "And just how were you going to do that?"

Irish drew his hand across his throat and said, "A tried and true method."

"You mean you were going to kill everyone."

They both nodded. But before Benny could speak Irish jumped in, "there was only supposed to be two people. But the place kept growing and growing and all those talks kinda' got to us...

Goldie interrupted, " and we liked it here."

Irish smiled, " we ain't hurting anybody now and we both feel a lot better about everything and we don't want you to tell Albert and you are talking to two of the holiest men you every met."

Goldie added, "Depending on who you met."

Benny sat there stunned. His eyes were tearing up.

Irish said, "we can't hurt anybody now."

Goldie said " we are learning to love people."

* *

The three men sat in silence. Nobody could speak. Then they all rose together and hugged each other.

* *

BABY- BACK IN THE CITY

Baby was pissed off at Dave. He had left her with nothing and when she called the advertising agency to check on him she learned he had taken a leave of absence. When she visited the agency to find out what the heck the 'leave of absence' was all about – every body she stopped in the halls told her they had no idea of why Dave had taken a leave. At least she came dressed to make an impression on one of these handsome boys – she would find out. She zeroed in on a 40 year old with a wedding band on. She followed him from the water fountain to an office door. She adjusted her clothing and pulled everything she could tight as possible and opened his door and walked in. The target was just shedding his jacket and about to sit down.

She said, "Oh, excuse me. I'm not sure I'm in the right office."

The target answered, as he turned over a picture of a woman on his desk, "Maybe I can help."

Baby smiled, she had got the right guy on her first try, "I'm so concerned Dave, my ex-fiancee, has disappeared, he worked here and now he is on leave of absence. I'm just sure he told someone here where he went." The target was examining various parts of her anatomy. He might be interesting Baby thought but that picture he turned was probably his wife and Baby never approached a married man.

"Well maybe I can help, what was his name again."

Baby told him the last name and kept praising him and his wonderful office as he made a few calls – he invited her to sit on the couch but Baby declined and she even declined lunch after he told her he was at that darn monastery he had talked about. Baby finally got up from her chair thanked the target for his help, kissed him on the cheek, and left. She got on the elevator quick and was out of the building.

Now she had to figure out a way to get to St. Sebastian's before Davey Boy got hooked by the holy rollers.

* *

ST. SEBASTIANS

After his encounter with Goldie and Irish, Benny felt that he had to talk with Albert about it. He wanted to talk about their conversion and their line that they were "two of the holiest men he ever met," but he felt he couldn't talk about their motive for coming here – that was too much.

He went to Albert's office and poked his face in. Albert was working at his desk on some papers and Benny asked, "could I have a few minutes?"

"Come in and sit down."

Benny thought of the ad he had seen in the magazine asking him if he was "BORED" and the things that had happened since that time. He felt better than he had ever felt in his life. He felt he really had a purpose and what part religion played in his life. Albert told him he was always this way he just had not adjusted the focus correctly. Now he felt focused. And the difference in his life that prayer had made. At one time Benny thought that prayer was something you knelt down for.. Now he understood prayer was the whole enchilada which you just lived and once in a while you could kneel down if you wanted to. And there in front of him was the guy who made it all begin to happen, Albert.

"I'm glad you came by, Benny. There is some disturbing news. I guess you could even call it bad news if you wanted to."

Benny thought bad news – if he told him about Goldie and Irish's master plan that would top his bad news – but he wasn't going to.

"I have a friend who helps me with decisions and he lives in Rome."

* *

ANGEL AND "FAMILY" ON THE WAY

" I know I said bring a lunch. But not a banquet for 50 people." Angel was looking at the food that Claudia had amassed in front of the Limo.

"Aunt Clara said we shouldn't get hungry."

Angel watched as Hugo loaded the Limo with four picnic baskets. Hans, the architect, was there with his neat briefcase bulging with plans and papers. Angel was rapidly coming to a decision – he was going to get Goldie and Irish out of that place and kill Aunt Clara's plans to give the architect Hans a job so he could marry her daughter, Claudia. The whole thing had just gone too far.

They all got in the Limo Angel had rented and Hugo drove them off.

BIG LEO

In another part of Town Big Leo was fuming. Fiddler was with him and suffering the words of a really mad Leo.

"You fell in an open grave?"

"But it didn't stop me from getting the poppers to Felix and Marko. They have probably got them all set and monks are going to start falling any time real soon."

Leo's wife was back from Atlantic City and smiling – she hit the jackpot on a penny machine and was so excited over winning $97.00 that she forgot about the 2 grand she lost on the ten cent machines.

Leo looked at Fiddler. He was not feeling right about the whole thing. One thing he knew that Fiddler did not know was the stupidity of Felix and Marko. He knew these two had difficulty spelling their own names. He should have whacked them right away instead of listening to their scheme to become Monks. "Get the car out. We're going to make sure those two monks know what they're doing,"

* *

Baby was on a bus. She hated riding buses. This bus to the Catskills was particularly annoying. Most of the riders were Jewish men dressed in black - with long beards. She had nobody to hit on – she surmised they were all staunch believers and they didn't know about hitting on a girl with one of the best figures on the east coast – at least that's what David told her once and he was in advertising. She did notice a bit of a twinkle in one of the very much older men – but she thought it best to leave him alone. He was gazing at her legs and she moved them away from his view, but they landed in direct sight of another guy – a little younger maybe – but she had paid her own way for the bus ride and she could take it easy. She would see what happens later on.

It was late morning and Albert was finishing his session with the boys. He had tried working on prayer again – it seemed to him that he always worked on prayer. In the time his novices had been with him he found that prayer was probably the best way to keep them interested. Not that they prayed an excessive amount but at least they had an idea of what it was, Parables and Prophets tended to confuse them. They followed Jesus' life fairly well – but morals was a mystery. He had found that studying morals even when he was a novice were difficult and almost impossible to put in neat packages of learning. Striving to understand religion and what it was – was almost impossible for the boys. Except Benny. Benny was growing everyday into a real working novice whom he thought would find it easy to step into a school of theology and become a 100% certified and ordained priest one day.

"Ask and thou shalt receive. I ask but don't receive. How about that Albert?"

It was Irish talking. Albert cowered and wanted to hide. All the 'class' was probably wondering the same thing and he had to answer it.

"Well, Irish, it's like this. If you pray for something like a..."

Felix piped up with "A million bucks."

Marko offered "A knockout woman."

Goldie kept nodding at all the suggestions, "yeah those are the kind of things I always pray for. And Look at me. No girl friend. No million bucks. When do I receive?"

Benny said "Let me answer, Albert."

Albert felt a load drop from his shoulders, "Sure, Benny, you answer the questions."

Benny went to the front of the little class room and leaned against Albert's desk. "It's like this. Your prayers are always answered.

We've talked about this before – but not the way you want them.

The reason we ask for a million dollars is that we think it will make us happier. Wrong. You are happier now because you have in your head all the good feelings that a million dollars would try to give you. You have it here – a good life – square meals – and most of all no threats from the outside. You are loved here and respected. Think about it . You once had to wake up every morning and figure out who was gonna' get you and who you were gonna' get. No more. You wake up in the morning and can relax – do a little physical work, have a good meal, watch the trees and the flowers and the birds. Then you have a chance to listen to Father Albert tell us about God. So you actually got a million dollar life without the hassle of the actual money. Think about it."

Dave took notes for future copy on St Sebastians – he could see the banner ad line 'A Million Dollar Job – Free."

They were silent. It had sounded good to them but they still wanted the jingle of coins and the feel of folded 100's.

Albert rose, " Thank you, Benny. Now we will all rise and say a short prayer "Glory be to the Father, the Son, and the Holy Spirit as it was in the beginning – is now – and ever shall be world without end. Amen."

They all left class. But doubt and worry still got to Marko, and Felix, and Goldie and Irish. And visions of Big Leo and Angel still danced in their heads.

The gate at the entrance to St. Sebastians was always kept locked – or at least it was since all the new recruits had entered. Albert had instructed Benny to always have a man available to open the gate for visitors . This was Mo's day at the gate. He actually didn't sit at the gate but rather in a room by the main door called the reception room. Whenever the front gate bell would ring he would walk the thirty paces to the gate and check on the visitor.

Mo was in the receiving room reading the paper. He loved the comics and his real passion was the New York sports teams.

He measured his fun by the victories of the Yanks, Knicks and Giants.

He was cursing a trade the Giants had just made when the bell at the gate sounded.

At the gate was the guy they had called Fiddler. He knew him from the old neighborhood. His name was Phil Knoblauch, or something like that, and as far as Mo knew he never played a violin.

"Hi Mo can you let us in this joint?"

"Sure Phil..."

"Not Phil, Mo, my name is Fiddler now."

"Who you working for now, Ph...er Fiddler?

"Big Leo. Two of his boys are doing time here."

"Doing Time?"

"Yeah, I guess that's what you would call it."

"You do time back down the road in Sing Sing – here you study to become a priest."

Mo was unlocking the gate.

"I don't think Big Leo knows that. I thought we was trying to break them out."

"They can leave whenever they want."

"Big Leo will be happy."

MO stepped aside and made room for Fiddler to get back in the car, a huge 1950 Cadillac, and drive through.

MO motioned them towards a parking spot on the side of the building and told Fiddler to sit tight.

"You can stay here I'll bring you Felix and Marko – we got regulations that I have to follow."

MO went back to his room and called Benny and asked him to get Felix and Marko. Big Leo wanted to see them.

Benny found Felix and Marko cleaning garbage cans and told them they had Big Leo for a visitor.

"He's waiting for you up at the front of the building."

Felix and Marko thanked Benny and said they would be right there.

After Benny left, Felix turned to Marko, " We could make a break for the river and swim across – someplace on the other side is Jersey -

and I have a friend in Jersey."

"You want me to swim across the river?"

"But Big Leo...?"

"And I can't swim - I'd rather be shot than be dinner for a bunch of fish – We at least got to hear what Leo says..."

"I know we're not getting a raise..."

They both rinsed their hands and headed for the front of the building to meet with Leo.

* *

The bus driver let Baby out in Stickville. The bus driver explained to her that Stickville was as close as they came to St. Sebastians. She was pissed and let the driver know it.

"They should've told you at the ticket office."

"But they didn't. So how the hell am I going to get there from here. I don't even know where I am...." The last part of her sentence dragged off as the bus pulled away. She turned and saw a small store and gas station in front of her.

She took one look at it and thought to herself "my body has always been my main commodity so body do your work."

She pranced into the store and smiled at all present – unfortunately everybody in the store was a couple of women and they were not going to necessarily going to jump at her body. She smiled at everybody and turned around and left – the garage next door has to have men – I hope, she thought to herself.

The two men at the station were charmed and their eyes almost fell out of their heads when she took a seat and crossed her legs with her very short skirt.

Ten minutes later she was in a 1989 Ford on her way to the monastery with her newfound friend, Billy.

* *

Angel, Hans, Claudia, and Jug (Angel's chauffeur) were hitting 65 along the Taconic Parkway north to St. Sebastian's. Angel could not believe that all this was happening to him. He was a hard working man. His father and mother had taught him to work hard, save money, and spend it well. His first paying job was a runner for the numbers man on the corner. The same place most guys in his profession started. Small nickels and dimes until now he could take bets in the hundreds of thousands if he had to. The down side of this whole thing was that it was considered illegal. He managed to overcome this little fact. What he thought he could never overcome was the people like Irish and Goldie whom he was forced to work with – they were stupid and probably the best of all the collectors who worked for him. He thought that nothing could be worse than those two guys, but now it was much worse, Claudia that lovely little girl who sat on his knee when she was in the third grade, had lassoed an idiot named Hans and he could hardly breath when they started to talk. How could Claudia have got herself so confused. The whole idea had been crazy and he was going to call off Goldie and Irish and forget about them. They stiffed him for a few bucks but he could live with it and they would be gone.

"Uncle Angel, aren't you excited." Claudia roused him from his day- dreams.

"Excited?"

"Hans is excited too. Soon he will be world famous for developing this barren part of the world."

She kept on talking but Angel had turned her off. He was back to dreaming how great life would be without Goldie, Irish, Hans and even old Claudia.

* *

The Cardinal sat in the rear of the 12 passenger limo and read his office. He never had time to read the prayers that priests (and cardinals) were required (maybe) every day. As a matter of fact he started reading from the first of last week and was bunching them up – he hoped to be completely caught up before he reached St. Sebastians. Father Harold, really Monsignor Harold, sat across from the Cardinals dozing. The task ahead was to solve the problem of who and what the women at St Sebastian's were doing there. He felt he had to go there in person. He hated the idea but the letter he received from the Cook, who was pleading the case of women workers, suggested that maybe she was campaigning for more than just using the women as workers. Harold had read into it that the women were participating in all the activities of the monastery. That was a real flag and required a lot of immediate attention. If the Pope ever found out about his chances for a cushy job in Rome would fall right out the window.

He spoke to the driver over the phone, "How much further?"

"About an hour excellency."

"God help us," he muttered to himself. Harold heard it and woke up. The Cardinal nodded, "Good rest Harold?"

"Yes, your excellency."

"I'm glad of that."

They both sat and looked at the country going by. Neither had much to say to each other. Both were thinking about the fact that they may have a rogue priest on hand who was doling out orders and ranks to women.

After a time the Cardinal spoke, "Harold, I have been thinking about your name. Is there a St. Harold? I never heard of him."

"Yes, your excellency there was a St. Harold. But I don't know whether or not he ever made it to the list of Roman saints."

"That's not good."

"Well actually I was named after my uncle Harold who definitely was not a saint at least not on this earth. He may well be residing in Heaven."

"But is there a Saint Harold. You know you should be named after a saint."

"Well the pastor of our church knew my uncle and he thought he was a saint and okayed my mother to name me after him."

The Cardinal was silent for a few seconds thinking about this. "But is there a real St. Harold."

"I believe so. He was old English. I remember we had a copy of this quote on our fireplace – "*In the sleep of the blessed grant, O Lord, eternal repose to the souls of Thy servants departed this life, Harold, last King of the Old English, his brothers Leofwine and Gyrth, his thanes, and all those who laid down their lives upon this field of battle for the Faith and England and grant them - ETERNAL MEMORY!*"

The Cardinal was quiet. After a short pause, "but that doesn't say he was a saint."

"But he died for the Faith and England."

The Cardinal, who was Irish, said, "I don't give a damn who died for England. I just think the monsignor who is my confidante and secretary should have a name after a saint in the Roman calendar."

155

"My mother slipped the name John onto my Baptismal record so I do have John – but I prefer Harold."

They drove for about ten more miles in silence, then the Cardinal spoke quietly, "Okay you can be Harold, but thank God for your mother and the name John.

* *

LEO WITH FELIX AND MARKO

Big Leo, Felix, Marko, and Fiddler were huddled on a bench under one of the Oak trees on the grounds. Leo was holding and examining a small number pad. "So you are telling me that if I press one of these numbers you have a popper – what the hell is a popper."

Fiddler answered, "it's a small bomb – very small. If one of our targets is near the popper he will go "pop" and he is gone."

Big Leo nodded his head and which button is which – if you saw a guy over by that door could you 'pop' him?

"Yes, Mr. Leo, I have that door covered," Felix answered.

"Which button is that door?"

Felix, Marko, and Fiddler were silent.

Big Leo asked again, "Which button is that door?"

Silence.

"Answer me."

Marko spoke, "We don't know. We forgot to make a...what do you call it...a chart – I guess."

" You stupid clowns – this is crazy. We have to know which button to push so the 'popper' and go off at the target.

Felix and Marko nodded their heads. "We're sorry."

Sorry – you're sorry – you are supposed to come to this place get rid of the tenants and return to me with the deed for the property. You are not supposed to be running around with robes on and doing whatever the hell you're doing. You are supposed to go (and he pointed his finger) go bang, bang, bang, and leave."

Marko nodded his head, "I agree, Big Leo, but these are all nice people- we don't want to hurt them."

You had a job to do. Do the job and leave. Not get involved with the targets. And if you want to talk about nice people – I am the nicest person you have known - do you know why?"

"Why Big Leo?"

"Because I am still letting you live. And you have some stupid plan of popping people off." He threw the number pad into the woods.

BANG

The tree they were sitting under gracefully fell down. They all managed to get from under it and hit the ground.

Marko quietly said, "you must have hit the tree button."

* *

BABY ARRIVES

"Billy, you were a doll. Thanks for the ride. I can make it from here."

Baby and her ride were outside the gate to St. Sebastian.

She rang the bell.

MO came to the gate. He recognized Baby from the old neighborhoods but couldn't remember her name. "Can I help you?"

"You can let me in," she twisted her head and looked at him, "Don't I know you."

MO smiled, she was attractive in all the right places, "You look familiar but I can't remember your name."

"They just call me Baby."

"That's nice – Baby."

"I'm looking for my boy friend, Dave. He was supposed to come and visit here about months ago and he hasn't returned yet."

"Dave joined us."

"You mean, Dave, is going to be a priest?"

"Maybe.'

"You better let me in quick. I have to reason with that boy."

MO opened the gate and Baby came in.

"Where is he?"

"I'm not sure."

"What do you mean you're not sure. He is here isn't he? He better be. I have had the most horrible experience of my life on a bus – all eyes kept staring at me."

MO knew what she meant. Riding a bus from New York would be a venture with all the eyes on you. He fully understood, however, the reason for the stares.

"Follow me, Baby, We'll try and find him."

* *

ANGEL ARRIVES

Angel and his carload of dear family members stopped their car about 500 yards away.

Claudia was holding the rolls of Hans' drawings.

Angel shouted from the car, "How much time does he want to get the feel of the place?"

"Just as few minutes more Uncle Angel."

Angel shook his head. – He was angry, pissed, and ready to kill. They had to stop down the road from the Monastery so that phony nut who was leading Claudia around like a puppy dog, could get an idea of the approach to his great spectacular development. He had not told them yet that there was not going to be any development. There was not going to be a 50 million dollar piece of land for him to play with – his plan was to let Goldie and Irish tell him that the whole thing had fallen through. That way Aunt Clara would not put him out of the family – which after today he was sure he wanted to be out of anyway.

* *

Big Leo and his 'gang' were still brushing the dirt off them from the falling tree. The tree explosion had attracted Albert and Benny and interrupted their discussion on the future of St. Sebastian.

Benny asked, "What happened, Felix?"

Marko answered, "We was just sitting here and Bang this tree falls over and nearly hits us."

Albert shook his head, "You mean it just fell."

"That's right, Father Albert, It just fell."

Big Leo asked, "Are you a real priest."

"I'm real."

"You don't look like a priest. You got a sweater on and sneakers and jeans. Where's your collar?"

Benny asked, "When is the last time you saw a priest."

"They had one at Little Joe's funeral and he was all dressed up like priest."

"I am Father Albert. What is your name?"

"I am Big Leo."

"Is that what you were baptized?"

"Baptized?"

Benny came to the rescue, "what did your mother call you..."

"Well, she..."

Benny came back with, "When you were a little boy what was your name?"

"I was in school with the name Leo Jackson."

"Well, Leo, I am Father Albert, welcome to our monastery, St. Sebastians. I see you know our brothers Felix and Marko. They are doing well and I know they are enjoying themselves."

Benny's discussion with Goldie and Irish played in his mind. These two guys, Felix and Marko could possibly have the same reason for coming to St. Sebastians. And that was not good.

* *

MO finally found Dave in the gardens drawing pictures and he led Baby to him. She saw him and ran to him...

"Davey , honey baby, sweetums," she had her arms around his neck and Dave's drawing went on the ground and she looked, to MO, that she was about to throw Dave on the ground too.

"I'll leave you folks alone for...."

Dave stammered, "MO, don't leave. I want you to meet..." and she covered his mouth with hers and continued to kiss him...

"I think your friend has things under control, Dave, I'll see you later." And he left.

Baby was all over Dave..."why did you leave me, Davey, you know I'd miss you like crazy, and what are you doing all dressed funny, you're not one of those priests are you?" and she turned on him again like a tiger in heat.

Finally Dave lifted Baby's arms from around his neck and led her by the hand to a bench near the pansy patch. He settled her down and patted her head gently. She didn't want this. She wanted more of his body and she kept on groping him.

"Baby, you have to cut this out. You have to relax."

" I just want you back, Davey."

"Well, maybe someday, but right now I am finding myself."

"Find yourself? You're not lost. You're with me."

Dave sat beside her and she took his arm she cuddled her head against him and Dave sat there staring into space – this is not what I needed now, he thought, and how do I explain it...how?

* *

Rodney sat with Ma and he was helping make meatballs. Ma figured they might need as 100 since Mo had stuck his head in earlier and announced there were several guests for dinner,

Rodney was smiling big.

"What's the matter with you," Ma asked, "you look like you swallowed the canary."

"Swallowed the canary?"

"It's an expression for how people put on smug and 'I know somethin' you don't know look."

Rodney stopped with the meatballs, leaned back against the refrigerator and nodded his head, "You're right. I do know something you don't know and I think it's coming to a head today."

" You mean St. Sebastians is saved?"

" I wouldn't go that far but something is happening."

"Have we got enough meatballs."

"We'll have plenty."

They worked in silence for as few more minutes. Then Ma stopped Okay Angel Rodney tell me what's up or I'll scream."

Rodney's smile grew bigger and wider and disappeared.

The two girls came in. They looked around the kitchen and opened and closed doors, "Who were you talking to, Ma?'

Debra shook her head, "we could hear you talking when we got near..."

"I think I hear people in the night, Ma, is this place a little haunted... in the religious sense or something," Linda wanted to know.

Debra agreed, "I love it here but it is a little eerie at night."

Ma kept working. You'll have to set extra tables tonight. I don't know how many extra...in the meantime work on these meatballs."

* *

Finally Hans finished surveying all the land around the monastery and got back in the car. Angel kept his cool – he was sure he was going to wake up soon and this horrible nightmare would be over. The nut even took soil samples and drove a stake into the ground for soil samples. Soil samples? Dirt was dirt and the poor guy was soon to get the shock of his life. The car pulled up to the gate of the monastery and Hans clutched his heart in admiration of the property.

Jug got out and rang the bell.

Inside the doorway MO wondered what the 'H' was going on today. Every time he sat down the bell rang again. He went outside to greet the new visitors.

Jug was standing by the bell and he let out a loud "Let us in."

Mo replied, "We're not open to the public today – next Sunday."

"We're not the public – de' boss has got business here."

Mo stared at the car and it was big. "Business with who.?"

"Those two bums Goldie and Irish."

Mo got a little mad – "We have no bums here. We are people studying to become priests."

Jug smiled, "You may not think they are bums but they are.

Claudia jumped out of the car and approached Mo. She gave him a big 'Queens' smile and said it was important since they were doing a survey of the land for the future. Hans followed here with a bunch of papers and it did look a little official to MO.

He opened the gate and showed them where to park – on the opposite side of the building from Big Leo's group.

He said he would go get Irish and Goldie

Jug got back in the car and parked it where MO had pointed out. Claudia and Hans began walking and taking in with lascivious smiles dreaming what they would do with the place once they took possession of it.

Meanwhile MO found Irish and Goldie and told them about the visitors.

Goldie looked miserable, "This is it, Irish, we got to face the music."

Irish shook his head, " what the hell are we going to say."

" I don't know but it better be good."

Irish nodded his head, "my father used to say 'when all else fails try telling the truth.'"

"I'm not so sure Angel wants to hear the truth."

"That's all we got. Let's go."

The two sad 'monks to be' walked to their doom – or at least they thought for sure that it was.

* *

A VISITOR

Johnny came on a horse, wearing his beautiful Tom Mix hat. He was an authentic cowboy. He was born on a Montana ranch 27 years ago into a family of nine kids, him included. He was the middle child so he took it from both sides, He was six foot 4 inches in his stocking feet and about three inches higher when he had his Tony Lama boots on. He weighed 194 lbs and was lean and trim. His face looked like leather and his teeth were like huge pearls set off beautifully by the dark tan skin color, His eyes were brown and his nose was about as long as you could make a nose. It seemed to go from his forehead to his upper lip. His hands were long and gracious but gnarled from hard work and his long legs almost made a perfect circle when he walked.

He had attended Montana University and had degree in cattle management. After school he worked on his Daddy's ranch watching over the cattle and some of the crops. All around their ranch people were selling their land to diggers who were looking for coal and gold and copper. He hated the noises their loud machines made. He was almost forty miles from the nearest active digger he could hear their rumbling in the night air. And the night air was getting more and more filled with dust and smoke.

He couldn't believe how pure the air was in other parts of the country.

About three months ago after reading the ad in the sexy magazine about being BORED he won $5000 riding a bronco in a rodeo down in Bozeman. He spoke to his Daddy and Mom and told them he was taking the $5000 and heading East to join those people who were going to make his life less boring. Working on the ranch wasn't really boring but it left a lot of loopholes in his thoughts about life in general.

His folks offered to buy him an airplane ticket east but he wasn't about to leave his horse. He and Paddy (the horse) started out across the country. Along the way people stared at them and even laughed at them but he and Paddy could care less. He was an old fashioned cowboy who could lasso, ride a bull, and throw a calf.

* *

ANOTHER VISITOR

Ralph graduated at the top of his class in June from Blessed Sacrament High School. He entered Harvard in September. He had little trouble getting into the famous university and he loved it at first. The competition in class was exactly what he always craved. He had been so far ahead of the other kids at Blessed Sacrament that he had no real competition in anything.

Harvard was different. He realized that he was dealing with the cream of the crop from all over and he actually had to study hard. He was not used to being challenged so he studied day and night. He gave up people for the books. In four years at Harvard he had attended 1 Radcliffe Social – (which he hated) – saw 2 plays – went to 7 movies and ate in one of three restaurants every night. He went back home at all the school breaks and his family held him up as a trophy – he was all brains and not a social skill anyplace. The only consolation he found anyplace was sitting quietly and meditating. He had been taught to meditate by a young man who wore a babushka to class and was a devout follower of Buddha.

The Buddhist student left the third year and went to Tibet. He had advised Ralph to continue meditating and listen to his heart . Ralph did this but without the companion he just couldn't do it.

One afternoon on his way to consult with his Philosophy teacher he stopped at a Church. Ralph had not been in a church in several years (since Sister Mary of the Morning Star made him go just about every morning at Blessed Sacrament). He was not sure why he went in but he did.

It was fairly dark most of the light being generated by candles. But most of all it was quiet. He sat in a pew and began to meditate. And to his surprise it was working well. He could actually do it in the quiet and dark and he felt relaxed and refreshed. He started coming back to the church and many afternoons when the church was empty Ralph sat in the lotus position in the side aisle and meditated.

He graduated Harvard with honors and many head hunters tracked him down for major companies but he could not make up his mind what to do. His parents tried to push him into a major company and then another major company but he refused.

His younger brother showed him pictures from a sex magazine and as beautiful as they were Ralph was not touched by them. He was, however, fascinated by the ad which began "BORED".

* *

"Irish and Goldie, my two boys, am I glad to see you. You look wonderful."

It was Angel greeting the two of them from about ten yards away. Each in his own way was trying to figure out what was happening.

Angel opening up with machine gun fire was more logical than the hugs he was no giving to each of them.

"Good to see you, Angel." Irish slowly got it out and was almost disappointed when he didn't feel bullets in his back. This was crazy.

"Mr Angel, we are happy to see you, but you have to know the mission you sent us on has not yet been filled." And how the hell are we going to explain it to him Goldie thought. Angel was a man with a very low tolerance. As a matter of fact, Goldie did not think Mr. Angel had any tolerance at all. He was known all over Queens for a quick resolution to all his problems.

Angel smiled, "Aah boys I know you tried your very best, but I can understand that it was an awful difficult task taking over all this land."

Claudia almost screamed. "You mean, you don't own all this land Uncle.

"You heard, Goldie, the mission has not been filled."

"Never mind the mission – you were supposed to get this land."

"Well..I..."

"You have failed, Uncle Angel. All the plans for our future – your future - my future everything depended on this beautiful country side being turned into a wonderful project for all of us...now, What am I going to tell Hans, it will break his heart ,and all those drawings and Aunt Clara."

Angel blinked at the mention of Aunt Clara. "Irish, Goldie, explain to my lovely niece Claudia our problem."

Irish and Goldie stood and stared at this family side of Angel.

"Speak – one of you and tell little Claudia, what went wrong."

"You tell him Irish."

"Ahhh well it seems...you tell her Goldie. I'm not sure I can."

"Speak Goldie," Angel spoke loud and clear in the forceful and demanding voice that Goldie was used to.

"Well, it seems, Irish and I, had a slight altercation of money matters with Mr. Angel and he was about to take extreme measures to collect

when I remembered an old story...yeah, that's right an old story about when an order of priests and monks decides to call it a day then their property was...aaa...up for grabs.:

Irish came in, " Yeah that's right. We thought we were going to be able to grab this place since they only had one resident and he was not feeling good."

"But he got better of his illness and the place is not up for grabs."

Angel, Claudia, Hans, and even Jug stood and stared open-mouthed at Goldie and Irish.

* *

The bell at the gate rang and MO answered it. He had no idea who it would be...he stopped and looked. Outside the gate was a cowboy sitting on a horse. He must have gotten lost on his way to the rodeo in Madison Square Garden. MO opened the gate.

"Hi, mister, I was bored and I read your ad. I'd like to come in and try it."

"You mean you want to join our order."

"Yeah, me and Paddy, that's my horse, have 'rid' all the way from Montana to give it a try."

"You know this is a religious group?"

" I do. I been pretty religious all my life."

"That's a start."

"You just have to sleep one night under the big skies in Montana and you know right away that there has to be a God up there taking care of the whole thing. I don't know anything about the 'ifs' and 'ands'

and 'buts' of religion but I sure got a religion. The biggest problem I have of comin' here is that it didn't say anything about horses in your ad and my buddy, Paddy, has got to come with me."

MO ushered the cowboy on a horse in and with a smile went to look for Albert.

* *

Albert was on the opposite side of the building still listening to the woes of Big Leo.

"I am sorry I don't look like a Priest, Leo but I am. After Vatican II, the church made an attempt..."

"Vatican who?? I don't know what that is."

Felix said, "I do."

Leo turned to him, "You do what?"

Felix answered, "I know what Vatican II is."

Leo growled, "Where did you learn about this thing?"

"Here, Leo. We had classes in religion."

"What are you takin' classes for. I didn't send you here to go to school."

Father Albert turned to Leo, "You sent them here."

"Yeah, I sent them here. These two guys owe me and they came here to execute a plan."

"I'm afraid I don't get it, Leo, what plan were they sent to execute?"

169

MO came around the corner and called to Albert, "Father there is a cowboy at the front who rode his horse here from Montana to join us. I think you should meet him."

"Mr. Leo forgive me I really should go see this." He started to leave, turned to Leo and said, "I'll be back shortly, I think we have some things to clear up."

"Yeah you're right."

Albert left with MO and as they left he said, "all the way on a

horse..."

Fiddler was the first to speak after Albert left, "He seems like as nice guy."

Leo sank to the bench, "How many guys do we have to 'do' before the place is ours."

Fiddler said, "Let me count. We got to get Father Albert, Mo, Goldie, Irish, Dave, Ma, the two girls, and I guess that's it."

Felix added, "maybe the guy on the horse."

"A total of nine.," Fiddler said.

Big Leo was quiet. Everybody around him was quiet. He turned to Felix and Marcus. "You two guys cost me 15 long ones for the truck – I lost the package pickup for the day which was probably another 15 and I was ready to simply shoot you and be done with it. But no. No, you tell me I can make millions by owning and selling this land and this building which you are going to give me since you will be the last remaining monks after you knock off the one guy that is left. Except it turns out there is nine guys left. Now we got an epidemic of people we got to kill off which the authorities will unquestionably question." He paused for thirty seconds, "I am now going to be forced to think so all of you remain quiet for the time."

* *

"I am sure we can accommodate the horse. We have plenty of ground here and the original owners had horses."

Albert was stroking the horse and feeling at home with him. He was thinking this young man came all the way from Montana because of that one Ad. That was remarkable. He did seem very legitimate and sincere in his approach to studying at St. Sebastians. Albert was thinking that he had decided to retire and send Benny on to another monastery to study but now this young man was projecting a quality that made Albert think and wonder if he couldn't stay on a bit longer. He had the funds to continue another year or two.

"MO show Jack where the old barn is for his horse then get him a room upstairs I need to get back to Mr. Leo.

Albert turned to leave when the bell rang. He told MO to go ahead and settle Jack - he would get the gate.

* *

Ralph decided to follow the directions on the "BORED" ad. His father grabbed his heart and slumped to a chair – his mother fainted away.

When after their Sunday dinner he told the both of them he was going to visit a monastery with the thought of joining them.

After some smelling salts for Mother and a glass of scotch for his father they started in on him.

Father: Do you realize who that man was that had dinner with us and just left. He was the president and CEO and everything else with the largest financial company on the East coast. They gross over 700 billion dollars last year. 700 billion – not million and he likes you. He likes you. He wants you to work for him. Ralph he wants you. Listen to me carefully - He – wants – you. You would probably be starting at a salary over $200,000 a year with the chance of earning commission points for an additional bonus. I need another scotch.

Mother: I know you have always been a serious young man. You always liked the insides of churches. You loved the smell of candles.

When you came to Europe with me you loved those tiny little cells where monks lived – you always thought they were so cute – you walked all the way up that tower where the bells were and you loved it – you even liked the wooden rosary beads that cost a dollar and turned away from the mother of pearl ones I bought you.

Ralph: Mother and Father don't you see me just walking around here listening to the radio and watching television – eating potato chips – drinking cold soda – wondering all the time what to do next – hoping that something will happen. I believe something will happen if I join a monastery – I will get a purpose – I will be forced to help people and help myself – I have never been the most religious guy in the world but lately I have been visiting a church to just sit and be quiet and talk – I think – to God. It has made me happy.

Father: Sports cars, women, beaches, ski lodges, all...

Ralph: (Interrupting) All those things bore me. I am going.

The next hour Ralph left. He left behind roomfuls of 'things' and took With him only the very bare necessities.

* *

Albert got to the gate and swung it open. The car was enormous. It reminded Albert of those long cars they used for high school proms and weddings except it was black and not white. Albert walked up the car and the drivers window came down. A priest stuck out is head, "We're looking for Father Albert."

"I am Father Albert. What can I do for you."

The rear door opened and another priest got out. He held the door for the next person out. After a few seconds the cardinal came out.

Albert was stunned, "Your excellency."

The cardinal was not very tall. Albert thought he must stand next to short people whenever they took publicity shots. His hair was perfect and he knew that was no $15 hair cut. He was outfitted in wonderful clothes all designer perfect. He stepped out of the car and extended

His hand to Albert. For a brief second Albert couldn't remember if it was still protocol to kiss his ring. He decided against it.

"So good to meet you Albert. You have a wonderful place here."

"Thank you, cardinal – your excellency."

"It must be refreshing living in the country – here under God's wonderful trees and alll the flowers."

He stood by his large Cadillac admiring the world about him and Albert kept thinking about what was going on in the parts he didn't see. Leo was on one side of the building arguing with Felix and Marko about their becoming priests – or maybe he wasn't

arguing about that...either way Albert was not sure it was a good sight for the Cardinal's eyes. On the other side was Mr. Angel

and Goldie and Irish and Clare and Hans the architect.

"May we go inside?, the Cardinal asked.

"Of course, come with me."

Albert led the troupe of the Cardinal and two other priests (one was the driver) into the seminary. Albert opened the door and led them to a parlor on the right. He stayed by the door until the had all entered.

As the last priest sat down Albert heard a sound. He turned and there was Debra running up the stairs wrapped in a towel. Albert quickly shut the door and Debra spoke, " I'm sooo sorry, Father,

I forgot to bring up my laundry — I'll be right out of the way." And she ran up the stairs.

Trembling Father Albert slipped into the parlor,

"What was that, Father?"

"Nothing, Excellency, nothing."

"It sounded like a young woman."

The lunch bell sounded.

"What's that?"

"That is the bell for lunch. Would you care to stay?"

The Cardinal spoke. "We will be glad to stay."

"I'm not sure what we're having — we did not know you were coming today."

"If I always signaled my arrival people would always be prepared in a special way. Arriving without notice gives me a chance to see how things are really happening."

Albert thought 'really happening' Big Leo on the right, Angel on the left, Dave with his girlfriend in the back, girls with bare legs running up and down the stairs.

Albert led them to the dining hall.

Ma had made meat loaf and mashed potatoes for lunch. Albert called Linda over and told her of the added guests. She ran off and set places for the Cardinal and his party. Debra, fully dressed, came in and helped her. Ma exited the kitchen and approached Albert.

"Albert, Benny invited a man named Angel and his party of 4 to lunch to lunch, MO informed me that Mr. Leo and three extras, that Dave's ex-girlfriend had to stay, and now you tell me three more plus a cowboy — is this all?"

Albert smiled and told her that this was all. When she started to complain, Albert stopped her with, "Ma, this is the Cardinal and his Party."

Ma stopped – stared at the Cardinal – she genuflected – and kissed his ring and said "Your highness, I am honored."

The Cardinal, actually seemed embarrassed by the kissing of the ring, but he pulled himself up tall and said, "I can hardly wait to try your meatloaf."

Everybody drifted in and sat down to eat. Linda and Debra served them all and the meal progressed. The Cardinal and his party seemed to enjoy the meat loaf and mashed potatoes. Big Leo grunted through most of the lunch. The grunts grew a little louder whenever he got a close 'listen to' at how much Felix and Marko were enjoying themselves. Goldie and Irish relaxed – it seems their boss, Angel, was concerned only with the young lady, his niece, and her guy with all the papers, Hans. Albert did not feel they meshed too well.

Benny got up from lunch at once and went over and sat between Dave and the girl he was with...she was getting far too amorous for a lunch with the Cardinal.

Albert was searching his mind for some kind of protocol when you have a cardinal for lunch. Was he supposed to ask him to speak? Was he supposed to just sit tight and do nothing? Was he, himself, supposed to formerly welcome the Cardinals.   That was what he decided - he would rise and welcome the Cardinal.

He rose. "Your excellency, fellow priests, brothers, and guests we welcome all of you to our table. It may have been different, the meal I mean, had Ma, our cook, had notice of all of you staying for lunch.

Ours is a very small community, but we are as devoted to our work as much as anyone can be and our fervor makes us a big community..."

Benny never saw Albert like this. It was almost like he was knuckling under to satisfy one man.

Albert finished and there was polite applause. Benny was unhappy. He wanted to say something about a bunch of guys who were finding some sort of faith and belief in God here at St. Sebastians.

After Albert finished his brief intro the Cardinal stood. He dabbed his mouth with his napkin and spoke, "Best meat loaf I've had since my mother used to make it every Tuesday in our little home outside Newark. We loved that meatloaf and we cherished our Tuesdays waiting for it. Good job, Ma." There was a polite applause.

The Cardinal continued, "I look out here at the men studying to be brothers and I see a real cross section of economic means. I am happy and glad you have found your way to St. Sebastians…"

Rodney nudged Ma and whispered "Hold on – its coming."

The Cardinal took a sip of water. "These beautiful grounds which we all love are not being used to their full potential by the fact that there are so few of you…'

Albert quickly looked at Benny – Benny emphatically shook his head 'no'.

…"We have carefully examined the physical plant here and at one time to the conclusion the Church would be better served if St. Sebastians were sold and the religious moved to other facilities in the diocese." groans from the audience and words of "no" came from the audience.

Benny started to rise, he was tense, he wanted to say something

The Cardinal continued, "But after this visit I see St Sebastians on the edge of a breakthrough. Father Albert tells me you have grown and today have several young men aiming to become real workers in the vineyard of the Lord. With this in mind St. Sebastians will remain

Open and have the full endorsement of the archdiocese."

Applause came from all those gathered even Big Leo who applauded with a frown. Angel was all smiles he was thinking that the schmuck Hans was going to have to eat his plans and his 'lovely' niece Clare, would have to go back and live with aunt Clara.

Dave turned to Baby and whispered in her ear that he was staying and going to go through a period of discernment. Baby had no idea of what he was talking about but she set her eye on Fiddler and changed seats to be sitting next to him.

Ma served an assortment of fresh fruit covered with real, made from whole cream, whipped cream and everybody ate with a gusto.

After the meal Angel took Goldie and Irish to sit at a bench under a tree. His niece Clare was still running around with Hans as if this were a dream world and they didn't want to wake up. Angel watched them for a short time then asked "Has she got my blood?"

Irish answered, "It's according to how you are related?"

Angel shaking his head, " I ain't ever going to ask again 'cause I am afraid to find out."

Then, Angel turned to Goldie and Irish. "I know you fellas had my best interest at heart in scheming to get this whole set up in my personal name. But as you can see too many people are going to have to suffer, especially me, if that Hans guy ever gets his plans unrolled and working. So the both of you stay here, try to be good, give me your guns, and don't smoke."

Thanks, Mr. Angel, we will really try."

* *

Felix and Marko, on the other side of the building, sat with Big Leo who promised to relieve them of their debt as long as they stayed at St. Sebastians. Felix and Marko both nodded they would stay a long time.

"Give me your guns."

Felix didn't want to let go of his favorite toy, "Geez, Big Leo, I may need this."

"Felix, from now on you pray from the hip – not shoot from the hip."

They both handed over their guns. Marko handed over the cell phone, "this is the phone that controls the poppers."

Big Leo took it. "this is a little dangerous for you to be hanging onto."

* *

Ma met with the Cardinal who told her the girls were far too pretty and " a bit sexy" to be hanging around a seminary. Ma promised him she would send them home as soon as she got some replacement help.

* *

Jack, the cowboy, was out back in an old barn, making a comfortable spot for his horse, Paddy. He was rearranging some hay he found there and raking the place into some order.

Rodney appeared to him. He stood there for some time watching Johnny then he said, "good job, this old barn hasn't been used for 50 years."

Johnny stopped raking and smiled, "I believe ya' – this dirt has all got to be moved and those stalls nailed together." Johnny turned his head and looked at Rodney's clothes – he didn't look anything like a monk. "Do you live here?"

Rodney jumped up and sat on a pile of wood that used to be a stall, "I did for a long time. But you came here and you were a signal."

"A signal?"

"A signal that things are going to be all right at St. Sebastians and I can leave."

"I hope you didn't let me scare you off." Paddy neighed, Johnny turned to him and when he turned back Rodney was gone.

* *

Angel left with his group in his big car.

Big Leo left five minutes later. He sat in the back mulling his decision. How bad would it have been if they had started blowing up St Sebastians. All those nice people - he was almost happy, not about losing the truck, but that he had visited St. Sebastians. He opened the car window and hurled the cell phone into a lake they were passing.

The cell phone passed through the air and twisted its way into the lake. A small branch from a tree over hanging the lake scraped against it. Then when all the coincidences and tricks of fate are added up nobody ever knows why things happen. When that branch scraped by that cell phone there was a loud explosion – a burst of flame 100 feet high.

And the Cardinal with his entourage standing on the steps with Fr Albert watched his $95,000 limousine blow up – but completely.

Everyone stared and 60 seconds later there was a pile of ashes.

The Cardinal was dumbfounded. He turned to Fr. Harold, "what happened?"

For the first time in his life, Father Harold was forced to reply. "I don't know."

179

* *

After two train rides and three bus rides Ralph Newton stood before Albert at the gates of St. Sebastian.

Albert opened the gates still a shaky from the explosion and said, "Hi I'm Father Albert. Can I help you?"

"I'm Ralph Newton. I read your ad and I am bored out here. I hope you have a place for me inside – I want to join your order.

Albert replied, "Come in."

finis

* *